Evergreens

and other short stories

Jerome K. Jerome

Alan Sutton
1982

Alan Sutton Publishing Limited
17a Brunswick Road
Gloucester

First published 1891

Copyright © in this edition 1982
Alan Sutton Publishing Limited

ISBN 0-86299-011-4

Typesetting and origination by
Alan Sutton Publishing Limited.
Photoset 11/13 Imprint.
Printed in Great Britain
by Page Bros (Norwich) Limited

CONTENTS

EVERGREENS

They look so dull and dowdy in the sweet spring weather, when the snowdrops and crocuses are putting on their dainty frocks of white and mauve and yellow, and the baby-buds from every branch are peeping with bright eyes out on the world, and stretching forth soft little leaves towards the coming gladness of their lives. They stand apart, so cold and hard amid the stirring hope and joy that are throbbing all around them.

And in the deep, full summer-time, when all the rest of nature dons its richest garb of green, and the roses clamber round the porch, and the grass waves waist-high in the meadow, and the fields are gay with flowers, — they seem duller and dowdier than ever then, wearing their faded winter's dress, looking so dingy and old and worn.

In the mellow days of autumn, when the trees, like dames no longer young, seek to forget their aged looks under gorgeous bright-toned robes of gold and brown and purple, and the grain is yellow in the fields, and the ruddy fruit hangs clustering from the drooping boughs and the wooded hills in their thousand hues stretch like leafy rainbows above the vale, — ah! surely they look their dullest and dowdiest then. The gathered glory of the dying year is all around them. They seem so out of place among it, in their sombre, everlasting green, like poor relations at a rich man's feast. It is such a weather-beaten old green dress. So many summers' suns have blistered it, so many winters' rains have beat upon it — such a shabby, mean old dress: it is the only one they have!

They do not look quite so bad when the weary winter weather is come, when the flowers are dead, and the hedgerows are bare, and the trees stand out leafless against the grey sky, and the birds are all silent, and the fields are brown, and the vine clings round the cottage with skinny, fleshless arms, and they alone of all things are unchanged, they alone of all the forest are green, they alone of all the verdant host stand firm to front the cruel winter.

They are not very beautiful, only strong and staunch and steadfast — the same in all times, through all seasons — ever the same, ever green. The spring cannot brighten them, the summer cannot scorch them, the autumn cannot wither them, the winter cannot kill them.

There are evergreen men and women in the world, praise be to God! — not many of them, but a few. They are not the showy folk; they are not the clever, attractive folk. (Nature is an old-fashioned shopkeeper: she never puts her best goods in the window.) They are only the quiet, strong folk: they are stronger than the world, stronger than life and death, stronger than Fate. The storms of life sweep over them, and the rains beat down upon them, and the biting frosts creep round them; but the winds and rains and the frosts pass away, and they are still standing, green and straight. They love the sunshine of life in their undemonstrative way — its pleasures, its joys. But calamity cannot bow them, sorrow and affliction bring not despair to their serene faces, only a little tightening of the lips; the sun of our prosperity makes the green of their friendship no brighter, the frost of our adversity kills not the leaves of their affection.

Let us lay hold of such men and women; let us grapple them to us with hooks of steel; let us cling to them as we would to rocks in a tossing sea. We do not think very much of them in the summer-time of life. They do not flatter us or gush over us. They do not always agree with us. They are not always the most delightful society, by any means. They are not good talkers, nor — which would do just as well, perhaps better — do they make enraptured listeners. They have awkward manners, and very little tact. They do not shine to advantage beside our society friends. They do not dress well; they look altogether somewhat dowdy and commonplace. We almost hope they will not see us when we meet them just outside the club. They are not the sort of people we want to ostentatiously greet in crowded places. It is not till the days of our need that we learn to love and know them. It is not till the winter that the birds see the wisdom of building their nests in the evergreen trees.

And we, in our spring-time folly of youth, pass them by with a sneer, the uninteresting, colourless evergreens, and, like silly children with nothing but eyes in their heads, stretch out our hands and cry for the pretty flowers. We will make our little garden of life such a charming, fairy-like spot, the envy of every passer-by! There shall nothing grow in it but lilies and roses, and the cottage we will cover all over with virginia-creeper. And, oh, how sweet it will look, under the dancing summer sunlight, when the soft west breeze is blowing!

And, oh, how we shall stand and shiver there when the rain and the east wind come!

Oh, you foolish, foolish little maidens, with your dainty heads so full of unwisdom! how often — oh! how often, are you to be warned that it is not always the sweetest thing in lovers that is the best material to make a good-wearing husband out of? 'The lover sighing like a furnace' will not go on sighing like a furnace for ever. That furnace will go out. He will become the husband, 'full of strange oaths — jealous in honour, sudden and quick in quarrel,' and grow 'into the lean and slipper'd pantaloon.' How will he wear? There will be no changing him if he does not suit, no sending him back to be altered, no having him let out a bit where he is too tight and hurts you, no having him taken in where he is too loose, no laying him by when the cold comes, to wrap yourself up in something warmer. As he is when you select him, so he will have to last you all your life — through all changes, through all seasons.

Yes, he looks very pretty now — handsome pattern, if the colours are fast and it does not fade — feels soft and warm to the touch. How will he stand the world's rough weather? How will he stand life's wear-and-tear?

He looks so manly and brave. His hair curls so divinely. He dresses so well (I wonder if the tailor's bill is paid?) He kisses your hand so gracefully. He calls you such pretty names. His arm feels so strong around you. His fine eyes are so full of tenderness as they gaze down into yours.

Will he kiss your hand when it is wrinkled and old? Will he call you pretty names when the baby is crying in the night, and you cannot keep it quiet — or, better still, will he sit up and take a turn with it? Will his arm be strong around you in the days of trouble? Will his eyes shine above you full of tenderness when yours are growing dim?

And you boys, you silly boys! what materials for a

wife do you think you will get out of the empty-headed coquettes you are raving and tearing your hair about? Oh! yes, she is very handsome, and she dresses with exquisite taste (the result of devoting the whole of her heart, mind, and soul to the subject, and never allowing her thoughts to be distracted from it by any other mundane or celestial object whatsoever); and she is very agreeable and entertaining and fascinating; and she will go on looking handsome, and dressing exquisitely, and being agreeable and entertaining and fascinating, just as much after you have married her as before — more so, if anything.

But *you* will not get the benefit of it. Husbands will be charmed and fascinated by her in plenty, but *you* will not be among them. You will run the show, you will pay all the expenses, do all the work. Your performing lady will be most affable and enchanting to the crowd. They will stare at her, and admire her, and talk to her, and flirt with her. And you will be able to feel that you are quite a benefactor to your fellow-men and women, — to your fellow-men especially, — in providing such delightful amusement for them, free. But *you* will not get any of the fun yourself.

You will not get the handsome looks. *You* will get the jaded face, and the dull, lustreless eyes, and the untidy hair with the dye showing on it. You will not get the exquisite dresses. *You* will get dirty, shabby frocks and slommicking dressing-gowns, such as your cook would be ashamed to wear. You will not get the charm and fascination. *You* will get the after-headaches, the complainings and grumblings, the silence and sulkiness, the weariness and lassitude and ill-temper that comes as such a relief after working hard all day at being pleasant!

It is not the people who shine in Society, but the people who brighten up the back parlour; not the people who are charming when they are out, but the people who are charming when they are in, that are good to *live* with. It is not the brilliant men and women, but the simple, strong, restful men and women, that make the best travelling companions for the road of Life. The men and women who will only laugh as they put up the umbrella when the rain begins to fall, who will trudge along cheerfully through the mud and over the stony places, — the comrades who will lay their firm hand on ours and strengthen us when the way is dark, and we are growing weak, — the evergreen men and women, who, like the holly, are at their brightest and best when the blast blows chilliest — the stanch men and women.

It is a grand thing this stanchness. It is the difference between a dog and a sheep — between a man and an oyster.

Women, as a rule, are stancher than men. There are women that you feel you could rely upon to the death. But very few men indeed have this dog-like virtue. Men, taking them generally, are more like cats. You may live with them and call them yours for twenty years, but you can never feel *quite* sure of them. You never know exactly what they are thinking of. You never feel easy in your mind as to the result of the next-door neighbour's laying down a Brussels carpet in his kitchen.

We have no school for the turning-out of stanch men in this nineteenth century. In the old, earnest times, War made men stanch and true to each other. We have learnt up a good many glib phrases about the wickedness of war and we thank God that we live in these peaceful trading times, wherein we can — and do — devote the whole of our thoughts and energies to robbing and cheating and swindling one another, — to "doing" our friends, and overcoming our enemies by trickery and lies, — wherein, undisturbed by the wicked ways of fighting men, we can cultivate to better perfection the "smartness", the craft, and the cunning, and all the other "business-like" virtues on which we so pride ourselves, and which were so neglected and treated with so little respect in the bad old age of violence, when men chose lions and eagles for their symbols, rather than foxes.

There is a good deal to be said against war. I am not prepared to maintain that war did not bring with it disadvantages, but there can be no doubt that, for the noblest work of nature, — the making of men — it was a splendid manufactory. It taught men courage. It trained them in promptness and determination, in strength of brain and strength of hand. From its stern lessons they learned fortitude in suffering, coolness in danger, cheerfulness under reverses. Chivalry, Reverence, and Loyalty are the beautiful children of ugly War. But, above all gifts, the greatest gift it gave to men was stanchness.

It first taught men to be true to one another; to be true to their duty, true to their post; to be in all things faithful, even unto death.

The martyrs that died at the stake; the explorers that fought with Nature and opened up the world for us; the reformers (they had to do something more than talk in those days) who won for us our liberties; the men who gave their lives to science and art, when science and art brought, not as now, fame and fortune, but shame and penury, — they sprang from the loins of the rugged men who had learnt, on many a grim battle-field, to laugh at pain and death, who had had it hammered into them, with many a hard blow, that the whole duty of a man in this world is to be true to his trust, and fear not.

Do you remember the story of the old Viking who had been converted to Christianity, and who, just as they were about, with much joy, to baptise him, paused and asked; "But what — if this, as you tell me, is the only way to the true Valhalla — what has become of my comrades, my friends who are dead, who died in the old faith — where are they?"

The priests, confused, replied there could be no doubt those unfortunate folk had gone to a place they would rather not mention.

"Then," said the old warrior, stepping back, "I will not be baptised. I will go along with my own people."

He had lived with them, fought beside them; they were his people. He would stand by them to the end — of eternity. Most assuredly, a very shocking old Viking! But I think it might be worth while giving up our civilisation and our culture, to get back to the days when they made men like that.

The only reminder of such times that we have left us now, is the bull dog; and he is fast dying-out — the pity of it! What a splendid old dog he is! so grim, so silent, so stanch; so terrible, when he has got his idea of his duty clear before him; so absurdly meek, when it is only himself that is concerned.

He is the gentlest, too, and the most lovable of all dogs. He does not look it. The sweetness of his disposition would not strike the casual observer at first glance. He resembles the gentleman spoken of in the oft-quoted stanza:

> "'E's all right when yer knows 'im,
>   But yer've got to know 'im fust."

The first time I ever met a bull-dog — to speak to, that is — was many years ago. We were lodging down in the country, an orphan friend of mine, named George, and myself, and one night, coming home late from some dissolving views, we found the family had gone to bed.

They had left a light in our room, however, and we went in and sat down, and began to take off our boots.

And then, for the first time, we noticed on the hearth-rug a bull-dog. A dog with a more thoughtfully-ferocious expression — a dog with, apparently, a heart more dead to all ennobling and civilising senti-ments — I have never seen. As George said, he looked more like some Heathen idol than a happy English dog.

He appeared to have been waiting for us; and he rose up and greeted us with a ghastly grin, and got between us and the door.

We smiled at him — a sickly, propitiatory smile. We said, "Good dog — poor fellow!" and we asked him, in tones implying that the question could admit of no negative, if he was not a "nice old chap". We did not really think so. We had our own private opinion con-cerning him, and it was unfavourable. But we did not express it. We would not have hurt his feelings for the world. He was a visitor — our guest, so to speak — and, as well-brought-up young men, we felt that the right thing to do was for us to prevent his gaining any hint that we were not glad to see him, and to make him feel as little as possible the awkwardness of his position.

I think we succeeded. He was singularly unembar-rassed, and far more at his ease than even we were. He took but little notice of our flattering remarks, but was much drawn towards George's legs. George used to be, I remember, rather proud of his legs. I could never see enough in them, myself, to excuse George's vanity; indeed, they always struck me as lumpy. It is only fair to acknowledge, however, that they quite fascinated that bull-dog. He walked over and criticised them with the air of a long-baffled connoisseur who had at last found his ideal. At the termination of his inspection he distinctly smiled.

George, who at that time was modest and bashful blushed and drew them up on to the chair. On the dog's displaying a desire to follow them, George moved up on to the table, and squatted there in the middle, nursing his knees.

George's legs being lost to him, the dog appeared inclined to console himself with mine. I went and sat beside George on the table.

Sitting with your feet drawn up in front of you, on a small and rickety one-legged table, is a most trying exercise, especially if you are not used to it. George and I both felt our position keenly. We did not like to call out for help, and bring the family down. We were proud young men, and we feared lest, to the unsympathetic eye of the comparative stranger, the spectacle we should present might not prove imposing.

So we sat on in silence for about half-an-hour, the dog keeping a reproachful eye upon us from the nearest chair, and displaying elephantine delight whenever we made any movement suggestive of climbing down.

At the end of the half-hour we discussed the advisability of "chancing it," but decided not to. "We should never," George said, "confound foolhardiness with courage."

"Courage," he continued, — George had quite a gift for maxims, – "Courage is the wisdom of manhood; foolhardiness, the folly of youth."

He said that to get down from the table while that dog remained in the room, would clearly prove us to be possessed of the latter quality; so we restrained ourselves, and sat on.

We sat on for over an hour, by which time, having both grown careless of life and indifferent to the voice of Wisdom, we did "chance it;" and, throwing the table-cloth over our would-be murderer, charged for the door and got out.

The next morning we complained to our landlady of her carelessness in leaving wild beasts about the place, and we gave her a brief, if not exactly truthful, history of the business.

Instead of the tender womanly sympathy we had expected, the old lady sat down in the easy chair and burst out laughing.

"What! old Boozer?" she exclaimed; "you was afraid of old Boozer! Why, bless you, he wouldn't hurt a worm! He ain't got a tooth in his head, he ain't: we has to feed him with a spoon; and I'm sure the way the cat chivies him about must be enough to make his life a burden to him. I expect he wanted you to nurse him; he's used to being nursed."

And that was the brute that had kept us sitting on a table, with our boots off, for over an hour on a chilly night!

Another bull-dog exhibition that occurs to me was one given by my uncle. He had had a bull-dog — a young one — given to him by a friend. It was a grand dog, so his friend had told him; all it wanted was training — it had not been properly trained. My uncle did not profess to know much about the training of bull-dogs; but it seemed a simple enough matter, so he thanked the man, and took his prize home at the end of a rope.

"Have we got to live in the house with *this*?" asked my aunt, indignantly, coming into the room about an hour after the dog's advent, followed by the quadruped himself, wearing an idiotically self-satisfied air.

"That!" exclaimed my uncle, in astonishment; "why, it's a splendid dog. His father was honourably mentioned only last year at the Aquarium."

"Ah, well, all I can say is that his son isn't going the way to get honourably mentioned in this neighbourhood," replied my aunt, with bitterness: "he's just finished killing poor Mrs. McSlanger's cat, if you want to know what he has been doing. And a pretty row there'll be about it, too!"

"Can't we hush it up?" said my uncle.

"Hush it up!" retorted my aunt. "If you'd heard the row, you wouldn't sit there and talk like a fool."

"And if you'll take my advice," added my aunt, "you'll set to work on this 'training', or whatever it is, that has got to be done to the dog, before any human life is lost."

My uncle was too busy to devote any time to the dog for the next day or so, and all that could be done was to keep the animal carefully confined to the house.

And a nice time we had with him! It was not that the animal was bad-hearted. He meant well: he tried to do his duty. What was wrong with him was that he was too hard-working. He wanted to do too much. He started with an exaggerated and totally erroneous notion of his duties and responsibilities. His idea was that he had been brought into the house for the purpose of preventing any living human soul from coming near it, and of preventing any person who might by chance have managed to slip in from ever again leaving it.

We endeavoured to induce him to take a less exalted view of his position, but in vain. That was the conception he had formed in his own mind concerning his earthly task, and that conception he insisted on living up to with, what appeared to us to be, unnecessary conscientiousness.

He so effectually frightened away all the tradespeople, that they at last refused to even enter the gate. All that they would do was to bring their goods and drop them over the fence into the front garden, from where we had to go and fetch them as we wanted them.

"I wish you'd run into the garden," my aunt would say to me

— I was stopping with them at the time, — "and see if you can find any sugar; I think there's some under the big rose-bush. If not, you'd better go to Jones's and order some."

And, on the cook's inquiring what she should get ready for lunch, my aunt would say:

"Well, I'm sure, Jane, I hardly know. What have we? Are there any chops in the garden, or was it a bit of steak that I noticed on the lawn?"

On the second afternoon the plumbers came to do a little job to the kitchen boiler. The dog, being engaged at the time in the front of the house, driving away the postman, did not notice their arrival. He was broken-hearted at finding them there when he got downstairs, and evidently blamed himself most bitterly. Still, there they were, all owing to his carelessness, and the only thing to be done now was to see that they did not escape.

There were three plumbers (it always takes three plumbers to do a job: the first man comes on ahead to tell you that the second man will be there soon, the second man comes to say that he can't stop, and the third man follows to ask if the first man has been there); and that faithful, dumb animal kept them pinned in the kitchen — fancy wanting to keep plumbers in a house longer than is absolutely necessary! — for five hours, until my uncle came home; and the bill ran: "Self and two men engaged six hours, repairing boiler-tap, 18s; materials, 2d. — total 18s. 2d."

He took a dislike to the cook from the very first. We did not blame him for this. She was a disagreeable old woman, and we did not think much of her ourselves. But when it came to keeping her out of the kitchen, so that she could not do her work, and my aunt and uncle had to cook the dinner themselves, assisted by the

housemaid — a willing-enough girl, but necessarily inexperienced, — we felt that the woman was being subjected to persecution.

My uncle, after this, decided that the dog's training must be no longer neglected. The man next door but one always talked as if he knew a lot about sporting matters, and to him my uncle went for advice as to how to set about it.

"Oh yes," said the man, cheerfully, "very simple thing, training a bull-dog. Wants patience, that's all."

"Oh, that will be all right," said my uncle; "it can't want much more than living in the same house with him before he's trained does. How do you start?"

"Well, I'll tell you," said the next-door-but-one man. "You take him up into a room where there's not much furniture, and you shut the door and bolt it."

"Quite so, — well, the moment you have knocked him down, he will jump up and go for you again. You must knock him down again; and you must keep on doing this until the dog is thoroughly cowed and exhausted. Once he is thoroughly cowed, the thing's done, — dog's as gentle as a lamb after that."

"Oh!" said my uncle, rising from his chair, "you think that a good way, do you?"

"Certainly," replied the next-door-but-one man; "it never fails."

"Oh! I wasn't doubting it," said my uncle; "only it's "I see," said my uncle.

"Then you place him on the floor in the middle of the room, and you go down on your knees in front of him, and begin to irritate him."

"Oh!"

"Yes, — and you go on irritating him until you have made him quite savage."

"Which, from what I know of the dog, won't take long," observed my uncle, thoughtfully.

"So much the better. The moment he gets savage he will fly at you."

My uncle agreed that the idea seemed plausible.

"He will fly at your throat," continued the next-door-but-one man, "and this is where you will have to be careful. *As* he springs towards you, and *before* he gets hold of you, you must hit him a fair straight blow on his nose, and knock him down."

"Yes, I see what you mean."

just occurred to me that, as you understand the knack of these things, perhaps *you'd* like to come in and try *your* hand on the dog? We can give you a room quite to yourselves; and I'll undertake that nobody comes near to interfere with you. And if — if," continued my uncle, with that kindly thoughtfulness which ever distinguished his treatment of others, — "*if*, by any chance, you should miss hitting the dog at the proper critical moment, or, if *you* should get cowed and exhausted first, instead of the dog — why, I shall only be too pleased to take the whole burden of the funeral expenses on my own shoulders; and I hope you know me well enough to feel sure that the arrangements will be tasteful, and, at the same time, unostentatious!" And out my uncle walked.

We next consulted the butcher, who agreed that the prize-ring method was absurd, especially when recommended to a short-winded, elderly, family man, and who recommended instead plenty of out-door exercise for the dog, under my uncle's strict supervision and control.

"Get a fairly long chain for him," said the butcher, "and take him out for a good stiff run every evening. Never let him get away from you; make him mind you, and bring him home always thoroughly exhausted. You stick to that for a month or two, regular, and you'll have him like a child."

"Um! — seems to me that I'm going to get more training over this job than anybody else," muttered my uncle, as he thanked the man and left the shop; "but I suppose it's got to be done. Wish I'd never had the d— dog now!"

So religiously every evening, my uncle would fasten a long chain to that poor dog, and drag him away from his happy home with the idea of exhausting him; and the dog would come back as fresh as paint, my uncle behind him panting and clamouring for brandy.

My uncle said he should never have dreamed there could have been such stirring times in this prosaic nineteenth century as he had experienced, training that dog.

Oh, the wild, wild scamperings over the breezy

common, the dog trying to catch a swallow, and my uncle, unable to hold him back, following at the other end of the chain!

Oh, the merry frolics in the fields, when the dog wanted to kill a cow, and the cow wanted to kill the dog, and they each dodged round my uncle, trying to do it!

And, oh, the pleasant chats with the old ladies when the dog wound the chain into a knot round their legs, and upset them, and my uncle had to sit down in the road beside them, and unite them before they could get up again!

But a crisis came at last. It was a Saturday afternoon — uncle being exercised by dog in usual way, — nervous children, playing in road, see dog, scream and run, — playful young dog thinks it a gam, jerks chain out of uncle's grasp, and flies after them, — uncle flies after dog, calling it names, — fond parent in front garden, seeing beloved children chased by savage dog, followed by careless owner, flies after uncle, calling *him* names, — householders come to doors and cry, "Shame!" — also throw things at dog, — things that don't hit dog, hit uncle, — things that don't hit uncle, hit fond parent, — through the village and up the hill, over the bridge and round by the green, — grand run, mile and a half without a break! Children sink exhausted, — dog gambols up among them, — children go into fits, — fond parent and uncle come up together, both breathless.

"Why don't you call your dog off, you wicked old man?"

"Because I can't recollect his name, you old fool, you!"

Fond parent accuses uncle of having set dog on, — uncle, indignant, reviles fond parent, — exasperated fond parent attacks uncle, — uncle retaliates with umbrella, — faithful dog comes to assistance of uncle, and inflicts great injury on fond parent, — arrival of police, — dog attacks police, — uncle and fond parent both taken into custody, — uncle fined five pounds and costs for keeping a ferocious dog at large, — uncle fined five pounds and costs for assault on fond parent, — uncle fined five pounds and costs for assault on police!

My uncle gave the dog away soon after that. He did not waste him. He gave him as a wedding-present to a near relation.

But the saddest story I ever heard in connection with a bull-dog, was one told by my aunt herself.

Now you can rely upon this story, because it is not

one of mine, it is one of my aunt's, and she would scorn
to tell a lie. This is a story you could tell to the heathen,
and feel that you were teaching them the truth and
doing them good. They give this story out at all the
Sunday-schools in our part of the country, and draw
moral lessons from it. It is a story that a little child can
believe.

It happened in the old crinoline days. My aunt, who
was then living in a country-town, had gone out
shopping one morning, and was standing in the High
Street, talking to a lady friend, a Mrs. Gumworthy, the
doctor's wife. She (my aunt) had on a new crinoline that
morning, in which, to use her own expression, she
rather fancied herself. It was a tremendously big one, as
stiff as a wire-fence; and it "set" beautifully.

They were standing in front of Jenkins's, the
draper's; and my aunt thinks that it — the crinoline —
must have got caught up in something, and an opening

thus left between it and the ground. However this may be, certain it is that an absurdly large and powerful bull-dog, who was fooling round about there at the time, managed somehow or other to squirm in under my aunt's crinoline, and effectually imprison himself beneath it.

Finding himself suddenly in a dark and gloomy chamber, the dog, naturally enough, got frightened, and made frantic rushes to get out. But whichever way he charged there was the crinoline in front of him. As he flew, he, of course, carried it before him, and with the crinoline, of course, went my aunt.

But nobody knew the explanation. My aunt herself did not know what had happened. Nobody had seen the dog creep inside the crinoline. All that the people did see was a staid and eminently respectable middle-aged lady suddenly, and without any apparent reason, throw her umbrella down in the road, fly up the High Street at the rate of ten miles an hour, rush across it at the

imminent risk of her life, dart down it again on the other side, rush sideways, like an excited crab, into a grocer's shop, run three times round the shop, upsetting the whole stock-in-trade, come out of the shop backwards and knock down a postman, dash into the roadway and spin round twice, hover for a moment, undecided, on the curb, and then away up the hill again, as if she had only just started, all the while screaming out at the top of her voice for somebody to stop her!

Of course, everybody thought that she was mad. The people flew before her like chaff before the wind. In less than five seconds the High Street was a desert. The townsfolk scampered into their shops and houses and barricaded the doors. Brave men dashed out and caught up little children and bore them to places of safety amid cheers. Carts and carriages were abandoned, while the drivers climbed up lamp-posts!

What would have happened had the affair gone on much longer — whether my aunt would have been shot, or the fire-engine brought into requisition against her — it is impossible, having regard to the terrified state of the crowd, to say. Fortunately for her, she became exhausted. With one despairing shriek she gave way, and sat down on the dog; and peace reigned once again in that sweet rural town.

CLOCKS

There are two kinds of clocks. There is the clock that is always wrong, and that knows it is wrong, and glories in it; and there is the clock that is always right — except when you rely upon it, and then it is more wrong that you would think a clock *could* be in a civilised country.

I remember a clock of this latter type, that we had in the house when I was a boy, routing us all up at three o'clock one winter's morning. We had finished breakfast at ten minutes to four, and I got to school a little after five, and sat down on the step outside and cried, because I thought the world had come to an end: everything was so death-like!

The man who can live in the same house with one of these clocks, and not endanger his chance of heaven about once a month by standing up and telling it what he thinks of it, is either a dangerous rival to that old-established firm, Job, or else he does not know enough bad language to make it worth his while to start saying anything at all.

The great dream of its life is to lure you on into trying

27

to catch a train by it. For weeks and weeks it will keep the most perfect time. If there were any difference in time between that clock and the sun, you would be convinced it was the sun, not the clock, that wanted seeing to. You feel that if that clock happened to get a quarter of a second fast, or the eighth of an instant slow, it would break its heart and die.

It is in this spirit of child-like faith in its integrity that, one morning, you gather your family around you in the passage, kiss your children, and afterwards wipe your jammy mouth, poke your finger in the baby's eye, promise not to forget to order the coals, wave a last fond adieu with the umbrella, and depart for the railway-station.

I never have been quite able to decide, myself, which is the more irritating: to run two miles at the top of your speed, and then to find, when you reach the station, that you are three-quarters of an hour too early; or to stroll along leisurely the whole way, and dawdle about outside the booking-office, talking to some local idiot, and then to swagger carelessly on to the platform, just in time to see the train go out!

As for the other class of clocks — the common or always-wrong clocks — they are harmless enough. You wind them up at the proper intervals, and once or twice a week you put them right and "regulate" them, as you call it (and you might just as well try to "regulate" a London Tom-cat). But you do all this, not from any selfish motives, but from a sense of duty to the clock itself. You want to feel that, whatever may happen, you have done the right thing by it, and that no blame can attach to you.

So far as looking to it for any return is concerned, that you never dream of doing, and consequently you

are not disappointed. You ask what the time is, and the girl replies:

"Well, the clock in the dining-room says a quarter-past two."

But you are not deceived by this. You know that, as a matter of fact, it must be somewhere between nine and ten in the evening; and, remembering that you noticed, as a curious circumstance, that the clock was only forty minutes fast four hours ago, you mildly admire its energies and resources, and wonder how it does it.

I myself possess a clock that for complicated unconventionality and light-hearted independence could, I should think, give points to anything yet discovered in the chronometrical line. As a mere timepiece, it leaves much to be desired; but, considered as a self-acting conundrum, it is full of interest and variety.

I heard of a man once who had a clock that he used to say was of no good to anyone except himself, because he was the only man who understood it. He said it was an excellent clock, and one that you could thoroughly depend upon; but you wanted to know it — to have studied its system. An outsider might be easily misled by it.

"For instance," he would say, "when it strikes fifteen, and the hands point to twenty minutes past eleven, *I* know it is a quarter to eight."

His acquaintanceship with that clock must certainly have given him an advantage over the cursory observer!

But the great charm about *my* clock is its reliable uncertainty. It works on no method whatever; it is a pure emotionalist. One day it will be quite frolicsome, and gain three hours in the course of the morning, and think nothing of it; and the next day it will wish it were dead, and be hardly able to drag itself along, and lose two hours out of every four, and stop altogether in the afternoon, too miserable to do anything; and then, getting cheerful once more towards evening, will start off again of its own accord.

I do not care to talk much about this clock; because when I tell the simple truth concerning it, people think I am exaggerating.

It is very discouraging to find, when you are straining every nerve to tell the truth, that people do not believe you, and fancy that you are exaggerating. It makes you feel inclined to go and exaggerate on purpose, just to show them the difference. I know I often feel tempted to do so myself: it is my early training that saves me.

We should always be very careful never to give way to exaggeration; it is a habit that grows upon one.

And it is such a vulgar habit, too. In the old times, when poets and dry-goods salesmen were the only people who exaggerated, there was something clever and *distingué* about a reputation for "a tendency to over- rather than to under-estimate the mere bald facts." But everybody exaggerates now-a-days. The art of exagger- ation is no longer regarded as an "extra" in the modern bill of education; it is an essential requirement, held to be most needful for the battle of life.

The whole world exaggerates. It exaggerates every- thing, from the yearly number of bicycles sold, to the yearly number of heathens converted — into the hope of Salvation and more whisky. Exaggeration is the basis of our trade, the fallow-field of our art and literature, the groundwork of our social life, the foundation of our political existence. As schoolboys, we exaggerate our fights and our marks and our fathers' debts. As men, we exaggerate our wares, we exaggerate our feelings, we exaggerate our incomes — except to the tax-collector, and to him we exaggerate our "outgoings", — we exaggerate our virtues; we even exaggerate our vices, and, being in reality the mildest of men, pretend we are dare-devil scamps.

We have sunk so low now that we try to *act* our exaggerations, and to live up to our lies. We call it "keeping up appearances"; and no more bitter phrase could, perhaps, have been invented to describe our childish folly.

If we possess a hundred pounds a year, do we not call it two? Our larder may be low and our grates be chill, but we are happy if the "world" (six acquaintances and a

prying neighbour) give us credit for one hundred and
fifty. And, when we have five hundred, we talk of a
thousand, and the all-important and beloved "world"
(sixteen friends now, and two of them carriage-folk!)
agree that we really must be spending seven hundred,
or, at all events, running into debt up to that figure; but
the butcher and baker, who have gone into the matter
with the housemaid know better.

After a while, having learnt the trick, we launch out
boldly and spend like Indian Princes — or rather *seem*
to spend; for we know, by this time, how to purchase
the seeming with the seeming, how to buy the appearance of wealth, — Beelzebub bless it! for it is his own
child, sure enough: there is no mistaking the likeness, it
has all his funny little ways, — gathers round, applaud-
ing and laughing at the lie, and sharing in the cheat, and
gloating over the thought of the blow that it knows must
sooner or later fall on us from the Thor-like hammer of
Truth.

And all goes merry as a witches' frolic — until the grey morning dawns.

Truth and fact are old-fashioned and out-of-date, my friends, fit only for the dull and vulgar to live by. Appearance, not reality, is what the clever dog grasps at in these clever days. We spurn the dull-brown solid earth; we build our lives and homes in the fair-seeming rainbow-land of shadow and chimera.

To ourselves, sleeping and waking there, *behind* the rainbow, there is no beauty in the house; only a chill, damp mist in every room, and, over all, a haunting fear of the hour when the gilded clouds will melt away, and let us fall — somewhat heavily, no doubt — upon the hard world underneath.

But, there! of what matter is *our* misery, *our* terror? To the stranger, our home appears fair and bright. The workers in the fields below look up and envy us our abode of glory and delight! If *they* think it pleasant, surely *we* should be content. Have we not been taught to live for others and not for ourselves, and are we not acting up bravely to the teaching — in this most curious method?

Ah! yes, we are self-sacrificing enough, and loyal enough in our devotion to this new-crowned king, the child of Prince Imposture and Princess Pretence. Never before was despot so blindly worshipped! Never had earthly sovereign yet such world-wide sway!

Man, if he would live, *must* worship. He looks around, and what to him, within the vision of his life, is the greatest and the best, that he falls down and does reverence to. To him whose eyes have opened on the nineteenth century, what nobler image can the universe produce than the figure of Falsehood in stolen robes? It is cunning and brazen and hollow-hearted, and it realises his soul's ideal, and he falls and kisses its feet, and clings to its skinny knees, swearing fealty to it for evermore!

Ah! he is a mighty monarch, bladder-bodied King Humbug! Come, let us build up temples of hewn shadows wherein we may adore him, safe from the light. Let us raise him aloft upon our Brummagem shields. Long live our coward, false-hearted chief! — fit leader for such soldiers as we! Long live the Lord-of-Lies, anointed! Long live poor King Appearances, to whom all mankind bows the knee!

But we must hold him aloft very carefully, O my brother warriors! He needs much "keeping up". He has no bones and sinews of his own, the poor old flimsy fellow! If we take our hands from him, he will fall a heap of worn-out rags, and the angry wind will whirl him away, and leave us forlorn. Oh, let us spend our lives keeping him up, and serving him, and making him great — that is, evermore puffed out with air and nothingness — until he burst, and we along with him!

Burst one day he must, as it is in the nature of bubbles to burst, especially when they grow big. Meanwhile, he still reigns over us, and the world grows more and more a world of pretence and exaggeration and lies; and he who pretends and exaggerates and lies the most successfully, is the greatest of us all.

The world is a gingerbread fair, and we all stand outside our booths and point to the gorgeous-coloured pictures, and beat the big drum and brag. Brag, Brag! Life is one great game of brag!

"Buy my soap, O ye people, and ye will never look old, and the hair will grow again on your bald places, and ye will never be poor or unhappy again; and mine is the only true soap. Oh, beware of spurious imitations!"

"Buy my lotion, all ye that suffer from pains in the head, or the stomach, or the feet, or that have broken arms, or broken hearts, or objectionable mothers-in-law;

and drink one bottle a day, and all your troubles will be ended."

"Come to my church, all ye that want to go to Heaven, and buy my penny weekly guide, and pay my pew-rates, and, pray ye, have nothing to do with my misguided brother over the road. *This* is the only safe way!"

"Oh, vote for me, my noble and intelligent electors, and send our party into power, and the world shall be a new place, and there shall be no sin or sorrow any more! And each free and independent voter shall have a brand-new Utopia made on purpose for him, according to his own ideas, with a good sized, extra-unpleasant Purgatory attached, to which he can send everybody he does not like. Oh, do not miss this chance!"

Oh! listen to my philosophy, it is the best and deepest. Oh! hear my songs, they are the sweetest. Oh! buy my pictures, they alone are true art. Oh! read my books, they are the finest.

Oh! *I* am the greatest cheesemonger, *I* am the greatest soldier, *I* am the greatest statesman, *I* am the greatest poet, *I* am the greatest showman, *I* am the greatest mountebank, *I* am the greatest editor, and *I* am the greatest patriot. *We* are the greatest nation. *We* are the only good people. *Ours* is the only true religion. Bah! how we all yell!

How we all brag and bounce, and beat the drum and shout! And nobody believes a word we utter; and the people ask one another, saying:

"How can we tell who is the greatest and the cleverest among all these shrieking braggarts?"

And they answer:

"There is none great or clever. The great and clever men are not here; there is no place for them in this pandemonium of charlatans and quacks. The men you see here are but crowing cocks. We suppose the greatest and the best of *them,* are they who crow the loudest and the longest; that is the only test of *their* merits."

Therefore, what is left for us to do, but to crow? And the best and greatest of us all, is he who crows the loudest and the longest on this little dunghill that we call our world!

Well, I was going to tell you about our clock.

It was my wife's idea, getting it, in the first instance. We had been to dinner at the Buggles's and Buggles had just bought a clock — "picked it up in Essex," was the way he described the transaction. Buggles is always going about "picking up" things. He will stand before an old carved bedstead, weighing about three tons, and say: "Yes — pretty little thing! I picked it up in

Holland;" as though he had found it by the roadside, and slipped it into his umbrella when nobody was looking!

Buggles was rather full of this clock. It was of the good old-fashioned "grandfather" type. It stood eight feet high, in a carved-oak case, and had a deep, sonorous, solemn tick, that made a pleasant accompaniment to the after-dinner chat, and seemed to fill the room with an air of homely dignity.

We discussed the clock, and Buggles said how he loved the sound of its slow, grave tick; and how, when all the house was still, and he and it were sitting up alone together, it seemed like some wise old friend talking to him, and telling him about the old days, and the old ways of thought, and the old life, and the old people.

The clock impressed my wife very much. She was very thoughtful all the way home, and, as we went upstairs to our flat, she said, "Why could not we have a clock like that?" She said it would seem like having someone in the house to take care of us all — she should fancy it was looking after baby!

I have a man in Northamptonshire from whom I buy old furniture now and then, and to him I applied. He answered by return to say that he had got exactly the very thing I wanted. (He always has. I am very lucky in this respect). It was the quaintest and most old-fashioned clock he had come across for a long while, and he enclosed photograph and full particulars; should he sent it up?

From the photograph and the particulars, it seemed, as he said, the very thing, and I told him, "Yes; send it up at once."

Three days afterwards, there came a knock at the door, — there had been other knocks at the door before this, of course; but I am dealing merely with the history of the clock. The girl said a couple of men were outside, and wanted to see me, and I went to them.

I found they were Pickford's carriers, and, glancing at the way-bill, I saw that it was my clock that they had brought, and I said, airily, "Oh, yes, it's quite right; bring it up!"

They said they were very sorry, but that was just the difficulty. They could not get it up.

I went down with them, and, wedged securely across the second landing of the staircase, I found a box, which I should have judged to be the original case in which Cleopatra's Needle came over.

They said that was my clock.

I brought down a chopper and a crowbar, and we sent out and collected in two extra hired ruffians, and the five of us worked away for half an hour, and got the

clock out; after which the traffic up and down the staircase was resumed, much to the satisfaction of the other
tenants.

We then got the clock upstairs and put it together,
and I fixed it in a corner of the dining-room.

At first it exhibited a strong desire to topple over and
fall on people, but by the liberal use of nails and screws
and bits of firewood, I made life in the same room with
it possible, and then, being exhausted, I had my
wounds dressed, and went to bed.

In the middle of the night, my wife woke me up in a
great state of alarm, to say that the clock had just struck
thirteen, and who did I think was going to die?

I said I did not know, but hoped it might be the next-
door dog.

My wife said she had a presentiment it meant baby. There was no comforting her: she cried herself to sleep again.

During the course of the morning, I succeeded in persuading her that she must have made a mistake, and she consented to smile once more. In the afternoon the clock struck thirteen again.

This renewed all her fears. She was convinced now that both baby and I were doomed, and that she would soon be left a childless widow. I tried to treat the matter as a joke, and this only made her more wretched. She said that she could see I really felt as she did, and was only pretending to be light-hearted for her sake, and she said she would try and bear it bravely.

The person she chiefly blamed was Buggles.

In the night, the clock gave us another warning, and my wife accepted it for her Aunt Maria, and seemed resigned. She wished, however, that I had never had the clock, and wondered when, if ever, I should get cured of my absurd craze for filling the house with tomfoolery.

The next day the clock struck thirteen four times, and this cheered her up. She said that if we were all going to die, it did not so much matter. Most likely there was a fever or a plague coming, and we should all be taken together.

She was quite lighthearted over it!

After that, the clock went on and killed every friend and relation we had, and then it started on the neighbours.

It struck thirteen all day long for months, until we were sick of slaughter, and there could not have been a human being left alive for miles round.

Then it turned over a new leaf, and gave up murdering folks, and took to striking mere harmless thirty-nines and forty-ones. Its favourite number now is

thirty-two, but, once a day, it strikes forty-nine. It
never strikes more than forty-nine. I don't know why,
— I have never been able to understand why, — but it
doesn't.

It does not strike at regular intervals, but when it
feels it wants to and would be better for it. Sometimes it
strikes three or four times within the same hour, and at
other times it will go for half-a-day without striking at
all.

He is an odd old fellow!

I have thought now and then of having him "seen to",
and made to keep regular hours and be respectable; but,
somehow, I seem to have grown to love him as he is
with his daring mockery of Time.

He certainly has not much respect for it. He seems to
go out of his way almost to openly insult it. He calls
half-past two thirty-eight o'clock, and in twenty minutes
from then he says it is one!

Is it that he really has grown to feel contempt for his
master, and wishes to show it? They say no man is a
hero to his valet; may it be that even stony-faced Time
himself is but a short-lived puny mortal — a little
greater than some others, that is all — to the dim eyes of
this old servant of his? Has he, ticking, ticking, all these
years, come at last to see into the littleness of that Time
that looms so great to our awed human eyes?

Is he saying, as he grimly laughs, and strikes his
thirty-fives and forties: "Bah! I know you, Time,
godlike and dread though you seem. What are you but a
phantom — a dream — like the rest of us here? Ay, less,
for you will pass away and be no more. Fear him not,
immortal men. Time is but the shadow of the world
upon the background of Eternity!"

TEA-KETTLES

It is asserted by scientific men that you can take a kettle full of boiling water off the fire, and, placing it on your outstretched hand, carry it round the room without suffering any hurt to yourself whatever, unless, of course, the thing upsets.

It is necessary to be sure that the water actually boils, as otherwise you will burn your hand; and it is also as well to look and see that there are no hot cinders clinging to the bottom of the kettle. These two rules observed, the exercise may be indulged in with much success.

The explanation of the seeming phenomenon is very simple. The heat from the fire passes *through* the kettle and *into* the water, and thus, as soon as the water boils, the kettle, as anyone who has studied science and these sort of things will readily understand, becomes cool, and may be carried about in the way I have explained instead of by the handle.

For myself, I generally adopt the handle method, notwithstanding, and take a towel to it. I did try the scientific way once, but I do not think the water could have been boiling; and that, as I have explained, is a very important point, because, except when the water is actually boiling, the kettle is hot, and you are apt to say: "Oh! Damn!" and drop it, and the water splashes out all over the floor. And then all the folks you have invited into the kitchen to witness this triumph of science, *they* say "Oh! Damn!" too, and skip about in a disorderly manner, and flick their feet in the air, and rush out into the passage, where they sit down on the cool oilcloth, and try to take off both boots at once.

I do not know how it is, but I have generally found a certain amount of variance between theory and practice. I remember they told me, when I was learning swimming, that if I lay flat on my back, with my arms extended, and kept perfectly still, I could not sink — not even if I wanted to. I don't know why they should have thought that I wanted to; but they evidently considered that there was a chance of my trying to do so, and that it was only kind of them to advise me not to, as the effort could only result in disappointment and loss of time. I might, if I stopped there on the water long enough, die of starvation or old age; or I might, in the case of a fog coming on, be run down by a boat and killed that way; but sink and be drowned, they assured me, I could not be. For a man to sink when lying on his back on the water was an utter impossibility: they worked this out on a slate, and made it quite clear to me, so that I saw it for myself.

And day after day, I would go down to the sea and place myself on the water in that position in which, as I have explained, it was contrary to the laws of nature that I should sink, and invariably and promptly go straight down to the bottom, head foremost!

Then there is that theory of the power of the human eye, and how it will subdue cows and other wild beasts. I tried that once. I was crossing a field near a farmhouse at which I was staying; and, just when I had nearly reached the middle, and was about three hundred yards from the handiest fence, I became aware of the fact that I was being regarded with quite an embarrassing amount of attention by an active and intelligent-looking cow. I took it at first as a compliment, and thought that I had mashed the cow; but when she slewed her head round so as to bring the point of her left horn exactly opposite the pit of my stomach, and began to sling her tail round and round in a circle, and foam at the mouth, I concluded that there must be something more in her mind than a mere passing fancy!

And then it suddenly occurred to me that it was because of this very cow I had been warned not to go near this very field. The poor animal had lately suffered a severe mental strain, owing to having been deprived of her offspring, and had evidently determined to relieve her over-burdened feelings on the very first living thing that came fooling around.

Well, there I was, and what was I to do? I paused for a moment, wondering. At first I thought I would lie down and pretend to be dead. I had read somewhere that if you lie down and pretend to be dead, the most savage animal will never touch you. I forget the reason *why* it will not; I rather think it is supposed to be because it is disappointed at not having had the fun of killing you itself. That makes it sulky, and it will have nothing to do with you. Or else its conscience is touched in some way, and the result of the deed it has been contemplating brought home to it; so that it goes away full of thankfulness at having been kept from a great crime, and determines to be a better beast for the future.

But, as I was preparing to drop down, the thought struck me: Was it *all* beasts that felt this way when they saw a man shamming dead, or was it only lions and tigers? I could not call to mind any instance of a traveller having escaped from a Jersey cow by this device; and to lie down in front of the animal, if it were merely going to take advantage of your doing so to jump on you, seemed unwise.

Then, too, *how about getting up again?* In the African desert, of course, you wait until the animal has gone home; but, in this case, the cow *lived* in the field, and I should have to go on pretending to be dead for perhaps a week!

No; I would try the power of the human eye. The human eye has a very wonderful effect upon animals, so I have been informed. No animal can bear its steady gaze. Under its influence a vague sense of terror gradually steals over the creature's senses; and, after vainly battling for a while against its irresistible power, the animal invariably turns and flies.

So I opened my right eye to its fullest extent, and fixed it hard on that unfortunate cow.

"I will not unduly terrify the poor thing," I said to myself. "I will just frighten her a little, and then let her go; and I will, afterwards, return the way I came, and not needlessly pain her by crossing the field any further."

But what appeared so extraordinary to my mind was, that the cow showed no signs of alarm whatever. "A vague sense of terror" began to gradually — I may say rapidly — steal over one of us, it is certain; but that one was not the cow. I can hardly expect anyone to believe it; but as a matter of fact the cow's eye, fixed with an intensely malevolent expression upon myself, caused more uneasiness to me than did my eye to the cow!

I glared at her harder than ever. All my feelings of kindly consideration towards the brute were gone. I should not have minded now if I had sent her into fits.

But she bore up under it. Nay, she did more. She

lowered her head, slung up her tail stiff at right angles to her back, and, roaring, made towards me.

Then I lost all faith in the power of the human eye, and tried the power of the human leg; and reached the other side of the fence with the sixteenth of a second to spare.

No; it is not well to rule oneself by theories. We think, when we are very young, that theories, or "philosophies" as we term them, are guiding lights, held out by Wisdom over the pathway of life; we learn, as we grow older, that, too often, they are mere will-o'-the-wisps, hovering over dismal swamps where dead men's bones lie rotting.

We stand with our hand upon the helm of our little bark, and we gather round us in a heap the log-books of the great dead captains that have passed over the sea before us. We note with care their course; and, in our roll of memory, we mark their soundings, and we learn their words of counsel, and their wise maxims, and all the shrewd, deep thoughts that came to them during the long years they sailed upon those same troubled waters that are heaving round us now.

Their experience shall be our compass. Their voices, whispering in our ear, shall be our pilot. By the teaching of their silent lips will we set our sails to the unseen wind.

But the closer we follow the dog's-eared logs, the wilder our poor craft tosses. The wind that filled the sails of those vanished ships blew not as blows the wind that strains our masts this day; and where they rode in safety, we run aground on reefs and banks, and our quivering timbers creak and groan, and we are well-nigh wrecked.

We must close those fading pages. They can teach us to be brave sailors, but they cannot tell us how to sail.

Over the sea of Life each must guide the helm for himself: and none can give us aid or counsel; for no one knows, nor ever has known, the pathway over that trackless ocean. In the Heavens above us shines the sun: and when the night falls, the stars come forth; and by these, looking upward, we must steer, and God be with us on the waters!

For the sea of Life is very deep, and no man knows its soundings, and no man knows its hidden shoals and rocks, nor the strong currents flowing underneath its sunny surface; for its sands are ever shifting, and its tides are every varying, and for the ships upon its waves there is no chart.

The sea of Life is vast and boundless, and no man knows its shores. For many thousand ages have its waters flowed and ebbed, and ever, day by day, from out the mist have come the little ships into the light, and beckoned with their ghost-like sails, and passed away;

and no man knows from whence they came, and no man knows the whither they have gone. And to each ship it is an unknown sea, and, over it, they sail to reach an unknown land; and where that land lies none can tell.

The sailors that have gone before! who are they, that we should follow them? For a brief day they have lain tossed upon the heaving waters: for a short hour they have clung to their poor bark of Time; and on the restless current it has drifted, and before the fitful wind it has been wafted, and over the deep they have passed into the darkness; and never more have they returned, and never more, though eyes, washed clear with bitter tears, have strained to pierce the gloom, have they or their frail ships been seen. Behind them the waters have closed up, and, of the way they went, there is no trail. Who are they, that they should draw a chart of this great ocean, and that we should trust to it?

What saw they of the mighty sea, but the waves lapping around their keel? They knew not the course they had sailed; they knew not the harbour that they sought. In the night they foundered and went down, and its lights they never saw.

The log of their few days' cruise, telling the struggles and dangers of their ship as it sailed, among so many myriad others, let us read and learn from; but their soundings of this fathomless sea, their tracings of its unseen shores, of what value are they, but as guesses to riddles whose answers are lost? Do moles draw maps of the world for the guidance of other moles?

In all things do we not listen too much to the voices of our brothers, especially in those matters wherein they are least able to instruct us? Is there not in the world too much pulpit-preaching of this doctrine, and too much novel and essay-writing against that, and too much shrieking out of directions to this truth and of warnings against that; so that, amid the shrieking and the thumping of so many energetic ladies and gentlemen, the still, low voice of God himself, speaking to our souls, gets quite drowned?

Ever since this world was set a-spinning we have been preaching and lecturing, and crusading and pamphleteering, and burning and advising each other into the way to go to Heaven; and we are still hard at it, and we are still all rushing about as confused and bewildered as ever, and nobody knows who is right, but we are all convinced that everybody else is wrong!

This way, that way, not the other way, we cry.

"Here is the path, the only path; follow me, unless you wish to be lost!"

"Follow him not! He is leading you wrong!" says another. "I alone know the way!"

"No, no, heed neither of them!" says a third. "*This* is the road. I have just found it. All the roads men have gone by before have led them wrong; but we shall be all right now: follow me!"

In one age, by sword and fire, and other kinds of eloquent appeal, we drive men up to Heaven through one gate, and in the next generation we furiously chase them away from that same gate; for we have discovered that it is a wrong gate, and leads, in fact, to perdition, and we hurry them off by another route entirely.

So, like chickens in a dusty highway, we scuttle round and round, and spin about and cry, and none of us knows the way home.

It is sincerely to be hoped that we do all get to this Heaven one day, wherever it may be. We make hulla-balloo enough about it, and struggle hard enough to squeeze in. We do not know very much what it is like. Some fancy it is an exhibition of gold and jewels; and others, that it is a sort of everlasting musical "At

Home." But we are all agreed that it is a land where we shall live well and not do any work, and we are going to have everything our own way and be very happy; and the people we do not like will not be allowed in.

It is a place, we have made up our minds, where all the good things of the other world are going to be given away; and, oh, how anxious we all are to be well to the front there!

Perhaps there are others, though, not of the piously self-seeking crew, to whom heaven only means a wider sphere of thought and action, a clearer vision, a nobler life, nearer to God; and these, walking through the darkness of this world, "stretch lame hands of faith and grope," trying to find the light. And so many are shouting out directions to them, and they that know the least shout the loudest!

Yes, yes, they are clever and earnest, these shouters, and they have thought, and have spoken the thought that was in them, so far as they have understood it themselves; but what is it all, but children teaching children? We are poor little fatherless brats, let to run wild about the streets and alleys of this noisy earth; and the wicked urchins among us play pitch-and-toss or marbles and fight; and we quiet ones sit on a doorstep and play at schools, and little 'Liza Philosophy and Tommy Goodboy will take it in turn to be "teacher", and will roar at us, and slap us, and instruct us in all they have learnt. And, if we are good and pay attention, we shall come to know as much as they do: think of that!

Come away — come away from the gutter and the tiresome game. Come away from the din. Come away to the quiet fields, over which the great sky stretches, and where, between us and the stars, there lies but silence; and there, in the stillness let us listen to the voice that is speaking within us.

Hark to it, O poor questioning children; it is the voice of God! To the mind of each of us it speaks, showing the light to our longing eyes, making all things clear to us, if we will but follow it. All through the weary days of doubt and terror, has it been whispering words of strength and comfort to our aching heart and brain, pointing out the path through the darkness to the knowledge and truth that our souls so hunger for; and, all the while, we have been straining our ears to catch the silly wisdom of the two-legged human things that cackle round us, and have not heeded it! Let us have done with other men's teaching, other men's guidance. Let us listen to *ourselves*. —— No, you cannot tell what you have learnt to others. That is what so many are trying to do. They would not understand you, and it would only help to swell the foolish din. The truths he has taught to us, we cannot teach to our fellow-men: none but God himself can speak their language, from no other voice but his can they be heard, — "The Lord is in his holy temple, let all the earth keep silence before him."

The serious and the comic seem to be for ever playing hide-and-seek with one another in and out our lives, like light and shadow through an April day; and ofttimes they, as children in a game, catch one another and embrace, and, with their arms entwined, lean for a space upon each other before the chase begins afresh. I was walking up and down the garden, following out this very idea — namely, of the childishness of our trying to teach one another in matters that we know so little of ourselves — when, on passing the summer-house, I overheard my argument being amusingly illustrated by my eldest neice, aged seven, who was sitting very upright in a very big chair, giving information to her younger

sister, aged five, on the subject of "Babies: their origin, discovery, and use."

"You know, babies," she was remarking in conclusion, "ain't like dollies. Babies is 'live. Nobody gives you babies till you're growed up. An' they're very improper. We're not s'posed to talk 'bout such things — *we* was babies once."

She is a very thoughtful child, is my eldest niece. Her thirst for knowledge is a most praiseworthy trait in her character, but has rather an exhausting effect upon the rest of the family. We limit her now to seven hundred questions a day. After she has asked seven hundred questions, and we have answered them, or, rather, as many as we are able, we boycott her; and she retires to bed, indignant, asking:

"Why only seven hundred? Why not eight?"

Nor is her range of inquiry what you would call narrow or circumscribed at all. It embraces most subjects that are known as yet to civilisation, from abstract theology to cats; from the failure of marriage to chocolate, and why you must not take it out and look at it when you have once put it inside your mouth.

She has her own opinion, too, about most of these matters, and expresses it with a freedom which is apt to shock respectably-brought-up folk. I am not over ortho-

dox myself, but she staggers even me at times. Her
theories are too advanced for me at present.

She has not given much attention to the matter of
babies hitherto. It is only this week that she has gone in
for that subject. The explanation is — I hardly like
mentioning it. Perhaps it — I don't know, I don't see
that there can be any harm in it, though. Yet — well,
the fact of the matter is, there is an "event" expected in
our family, or rather, in my brother-in-law's; and there!
you know how these things get discussed among
relations, and May, that is my niece's name, is one of
those children that you are always forgetting is about,
and never know how much it has heard and how much
it has not.

The child said nothing, however, and all seemed right
until last Sunday afternoon. It was a wet day, and I was
reading in the breakfast-parlour, and Emily was sitting
on the sofa, looking at an album of Swiss views with
Dick Chetwyn. Dick and Emily are engaged. Dick is a
steady young fellow, and Emily loves him dearly, I am
sure; but they both suffer, in my opinion, from an over-

sense of modesty. As for Emily, it does not so much matter: girls are like that before they are married. But in Dick it seems out of place. They both of them flare up quite scarlet at the simplest joke even. They always make me think of Gilbert's bashful young couple.

Well, there we were, sitting round, the child on the floor, playing with her bricks. She had been very quiet for about five minutes, and I was just wondering what could be the matter with her, when all of a sudden, and without a word of warning, she observed, in the most casual tone of voice, while continuing her building operations:

"Is Auntie Cissy goin' to have a little boy-baby, or a little girl-baby, uncle?"

"Oh, don't ask silly questions; she hasn't made up her mind yet."

"Oh, oh! I think I should 'vise her to have a little girl, 'cause little girls ain't so much trouble as boys is they? Which would you 'vise her to have, uncle?"

"Will you go on with your bricks, and not talk about things you don't understand? We're not supposed to talk about those sort of things at all. It isn't proper.'

"Wha isn't p'oper? Ain't babies p'oper?"

"No; very *im*proper, especially some of them."

"'Umph! then what's people have 'em for, if they isn't p'oper?"

"Will you go on with your bricks, or will you not? How much oftener am I to speak to you, I wonder? People can't help having them. They are sent to chasten us; to teach us what a worrying, drive-you-mad sort of world this is, and we have to put up with them. But there's no need to talk about them."

There was silence for a few minutes, and then came:

"Does Uncle Henry know? He'll be her puppa, won't he?"

"Eh! What? Know what? What are you talking about now?"

"Does Uncle Henry know 'bout this baby that Auntie Cissy's going to have?"

"Yes, of course, you little idiot! — Does Uncle Henry know!"

"Yes — I s'pose they'd tell him, 'cause, you see, he'll have to pay for it, won't he?"

"Well, nobody else will if he doesn't."

"It costs heaps and *heaps* and HEAPS of money, a baby, don't it?"

"Yes, heaps."

"Two shillin's?"

"Oh, more than that!"

"Yes, I s'pose they're very 'spensive. Could I have a baby, uncle?"

"Oh, yes; two."

"No, really! On my birthday?"

"Oh, don't be so silly! Babies are not dolls. Babies are alive! You don't buy them. You are given them when you are grown up."

"Shall *I* have a baby when *I*'m growed up?"

"Oh, it all depends! And don't say 'growed up.'

You've been told that before. It's 'grow*n* up,' not 'grow*ed* up.' I don't know where you get your English from."

"When I'm grow*n*ed up, then. Shall I have a baby when I'm growned up?"

"Oh, bother the child! Yes, if you're good and don't worry, and get married."

"What's 'married'? What mumma and puppa is?"

"Yes."

"And what Auntie Emily and Mr Chetwyn is goin' to be?"

"Yes; don't talk so much."

"Oh! can't you have a baby 'less you're married?"

"No, certainly not."

"Oh! Will Auntie Emily have a——"

"Go ON WITH YOUR BRICKS! I'll take those bricks away from you, if you don't play quietly with them. You never hear me or your father ask silly questions like that. You haven't learnt your lessons for tomorrow yet, you know."

Confound the child! I can't make out where children get their notions from, confounded little nuisances!

Let me see, what was I writing about? Oh! I know, "Tea-kettles." Yes, it ought to be rather an interesting subject, "Tea-kettles." I should think a man might write a very good article on "Tea-kettles." I must have a try at it one of these days!

A PATHETIC STORY

"Oh! I want you to write the pathetic story for the Christmas number, if you will, old man," said the editor of the —— *Weekly Journal* to me, as I poked my head into his den one sunny July morning, some years ago.

"Thomas is anxious to have the comic sketch. He says he overheard a joke last week, that he thinks he can work up. I expect I shall have to do the cheerful love story, about the man that everybody thinks is dead and that turns up on Christmas-eve and marries the girl, myself. I was hoping to get out of it this time, but I'm afraid I can't. Then I shall get Miggs to do the charitable appeal business. I think he's the most experienced man we have now for that; and Skittles can run off the cynical column, about the Christmas bills, and the indigestion: he's always very good in a cynical article, Skittles is; he's got just the correct don't-know-what-he-means-himself sort of touch for it, if you understand."

"Skittles," I may mention, was the nickname we had given to a singularly emotional and seriously inclined member of the staff, whose correct cognomen was Beherhend.

Skittles himself always waxed particularly sentimental over Christmas. During the week preceding that sacred festival, he used to go about literally swelling with geniality and affection for all man and womankind. He would greet comparative strangers with a burst of delight

that other men would have found difficult to work up in the case of a rich relation, and would shower upon them the good wishes, always so plentiful and cheap at that season, with such an evident conviction that practical benefit to the wishee would ensue therefrom as to send them away labouring under a vague sense of obligation.

The sight of an old friend at that period was almost

dangerous to him. His feelings would quite overcome him. He could not speak. You feared that he would burst.

He was generally quite laid up on Christmas-day itself, owing to having drunk so many sentimental toasts on Christmas-eve. I never saw such a man as Skittles for proposing and drinking sentimental toasts. He would drink to "dear old Christmas-time," and to "dear old England;" and then he would drink to his mother, and all his other relations, and to "lovely woman," and "old chums," or he would propose "Friendship," in the abstract, "may it never grow cool in the heart of a true-born Briton," and "Love — may it ever look out at us from the eyes of our sweethearts and wives," or even "The Sun — that is ever shining behind the clouds, dear boys, — where we can't see it, and where it is not of much use to us." He was so full of sentiment, was Skittles!

But his favourite toast, and the one over which he would become more eloquently lugubrious than over any other, was always "absent friends". He appeared to be singularly rich in "absent friends". And it must be said for him that he never forgot them. Whenever and wherever liquor was to his hand, Skittles's "absent friends" were sure of a drink, and his present friends, unless they displayed great tact and firmness, of a speech calculated to give them all the blues for a week.

Folks did say at one time that Skittles's eyes usually turned in the direction of the county jail when he pledged this toast; but on its being ascertained that Skittles's kindly remembrance was not intended to be exclusive, but embraced everybody else's absent friends as well as his own, the uncharitable suggestion was withdrawn.

Still, we had too much of these "absent friends",

however comprehensive a body they may have been. Skittles overdid the business. We all think highly of our friends when they are absent — more highly, as a rule, than we do of them when they are not absent. But we do not want to be always worrying about them. At a Christmas party, or a complimentary dinner to somebody, or at a shareholders' meeting, where you naturally feel good and sad, they are in place, but Skittles dragged them in at the most inappropriate seasons. Never shall I forget his proposing their health once at a wedding. It had been a jolly wedding. Everything had gone off splendidly, and everybody was in the best of spirits. The breakfast was over, and quite all the necessary toasts had been drunk. It was getting near the time for the bride and bridegroom to depart, and we were just thinking about collecting the rice and boots with which to finally bless them, when Skittles rose in his place, with a funereal expression on his countenance and a glass of wine in his hand.

I guessed what was coming in a moment. I tried to kick him under the table. I do not mean, of course, that I tried to kick him there altogether; though I am not at all sure whether, under the circumstances, I should not have been justified in going even to that length. What I mean is, that the attempt to kick him took place under the table.

It failed, however. True, I did kick somebody; but it evidently could not have been Skittles, for he remained unmoved. In all probability it was the bride, who was sitting next to him. I did not try again; and he started, uninterfered with, on his favourite theme.

"Friends," he commenced, his voice trembling with

emotion, while a tear glistened in his eye, "before we part — some of us, perhaps, never to meet again on earth — before this guileless young couple, who have this day taken upon themselves the manifold trials and troubles of married life, quit the peaceful fold, as it were, to face the bitter griefs and disappointments of this weary life, there is one toast, hitherto undrunk, that I would wish to propose."

Here he wiped away the before-mentioned tear, and the people looked solemn, and endeavoured to crack nuts without making a noise.

"Friends," he went on, growing more and more impressive and dejected in his tones, "there are few of us here who have not at some time or other known what it is to lose, through death or travel, a dear beloved one — maybe two or three."

At this point, he stifled a sob; and the bridegroom's aunt, at the bottom of the table, whose eldest son had lately left the country at the expense of his relations, upon the clear understanding that he would never again return, began to cry quietly into the ice-pudding.

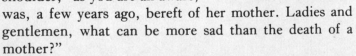

"The fair young maiden at my side," continued Skittles, clearing his throat, and laying his hand tenderly on the bride's shoulder, "as you are all aware, was, a few years ago, bereft of her mother. Ladies and gentlemen, what can be more sad than the death of a mother?"

This, of course, had the effect of starting the bride off sobbing. The bridegroom, meaning well, but, naturally, under the circumstances, nervous and excited, sought to console her by murmuring that he felt sure it had all happened for the best, and that no one who had ever known the old lady would for a moment wish her back again; upon which he was indignantly informed by his newly-made wife that if he was so pleased at her mother's death, it was a pity he had not told her so before, and she would never have married him — and he sank into thoughtful silence.

On my looking up, which I had hitherto carefully abstained from doing, my eyes unfortunately encountered those of a brother journalist who was sitting at the other side of the table, and we both burst out laughing, thereupon gaining a reputation for callousness that I do not suppose either of us has outlived to this day.

Skittles, the only human being at that once festive board that did not appear to be wishing he were anywhere else, droned on, with evident satisfaction:

"Friends," he said, "shall that dear mother be forgotten at this joyous gathering? Shall the lost mother, father, brother, sister, child, friend of any of us be forgotten? No, ladies and gentlemen! Let us, amid our merriment, still think of those lost, wandering souls: let us, amid the wine-cup and the blithesome jest, remember — 'Absent Friends'."

The toast was drunk to the accompaniment of suppressed sobs and low moans, and the wedding guests left the table to bathe their faces and calm their thoughts. The bride, rejecting the proffered assistance of the groom, was assisted into the carriage by her father, and departed, evidently full of misgivings as to her chance of future happiness in the society of such a heartless monster as her husband had just shown himself to be!

Skittles has been an "absent friend" himself at that house since then.

But I am not getting on with my pathetic story.

"Do not be late with it," our editor had said. "Let me have it by the end of August, certain. I mean to be early with the Christmas number this time. We didn't get it out till October last year, you know. I don't want the *Clipper* to be before us again!"

"Oh, that will be all right," I had answered, airily. "I shall soon run that off. I've nothing much to do this week. I'll start it at once."

So, as I went home, I cast about in my mind for a pathetic subject to work on. But not a pathetic idea could I think of. Comic fancies crowded in upon me, until my brain began to give way under the strain of holding them; and, if I had not calmed myself down with a last week's *Punch,* I should, in all probability, have gone off in a fit.

"Oh, I'm evidently not in the humour for pathos," I said to myself. "It is no use trying to force it. I've got plenty of time. I will wait till I feel sad."

But as the days went on, I merely grew more and more cheerful. By the middle of August, matters were becoming serious. If I could not, by some means or other, contrive to get myself into a state of the blues during the next week or ten days, there would be nothing in the Christmas number of the ——*Weekly Journal* to make the British public wretched, and its reputation as a high-class paper for the family circle would be irretrievably ruined!

I was a conscientious young man in those days. I had undertaken to write a four-and-a-half column pathetic story by the end of August; and if — no matter at what mental or physical cost to myself — the task could be accomplished, those four columns and a half should be ready.

I have generally found indigestion a good breeder of

sorrowful thoughts. Accordingly, for a couple of days I lived upon an exclusive diet of hot boiled pork, Yorkshire pudding, and assorted pastry, with lobster salad for supper. It gave me comic nightmares. I dreamed of elephants trying to climb trees, and of

churchwardens being caught playing pitch-and-toss on Sundays, and woke up shaking with laughter!

I abandoned the dyspeptic scheme, and took to reading all the pathetic literature I could collect together. But it was of no use. The little girl in Wordsworth's "We are Seven" only irritated me; I wanted to slap her. Byron's blighted pirates bored me. When, in a novel, the heroine died, I was glad; and when the author told me that the hero never smiled again on earth, I did not believe it.

As a last resource, I re-perused one or two of my own concoctions. They made me feel ashamed of myself, but not exactly miserable — at least, not miserable in the way I wanted to be miserable.

Then I bought all the standard works of wit and humour that had ever been published, and waded steadily through the lot. They lowered me a good deal, but not sufficiently. My cheerfulness seemed proof against everything.

One Saturday evening I went out and hired a man to come in and sing sentimental ballads to me. He earned his money (five shillings). He sang me everything dismal there was in English, Scotch, Irish, and Welsh, together with a few translations from the German; and, after the first hour and a half, I found myself unconsciously trying to dance to the different tunes. I invented some really pretty steps for "Auld Robin Grey," winding up with a quaint flourish of the left leg at the end of each verse.

At the beginning of the last week, I went to my editor and laid the case before him.

"Why, what's the matter with you?" he said. "You used to be so good at that sort of thing! Have you thought of the poor girl who loves the young man that goes away and never comes back, and she waits and waits, and never marries, and nobody knows that her heart is breaking?"

"Of course I have!" I retorted, rather irritably. "Do you think I don't know the rudiments of my profession?"

"Well," he remarked, "won't it do?"

"No," I answered. "With marriage such a failure as it seems to be all round now-a-days, how can you pump up sorrow for anyone lucky enough to keep out of it?"

"Um," he mused, "how about the child that tells everybody not to cry, and then dies?"

"Oh, and a good riddance to it!" I replied, peevishly. "There are too many children in this world. Look what a noise they make, and what a lot of money they cost in boots!"

My editor agreed that I did not appear to be in the proper spirit to write a pathetic child-story.

He inquired if I had thought of the old man who wept over the faded love-letters on Christmas-eve; and I said that I had, and that I considered him an old idiot.

"Would a dog story do?" he continued: "something about a dead dog; that's always popular."

"Not Christmassy enough," I argued.

The betrayed maiden was suggested; but dismissed, on reflection, as being too broad a subject for the pages of a "Companion for the Home Circle" — our sub-title.

"Well, think it over for another day," said my editor. "I don't want to have to go to Jenks. He can only be pathetic as a costermonger, and our lady readers don't always like the expressions."

I thought I would go and ask the advice of a friend of mine — a very famous and popular author; in fact, one of the *most* famous and popular authors of the day. I was very proud of his friendship, because he was a very great man indeed: not great, perhaps, in the earnest meaning of the word; not great like the greatest men — the men who do not know that they are great — but decidedly great, according to the practical standard. When he wrote a book, a hundred thousand copies would be sold during the first week; and when a play of his was produced, the theatre was crammed for five hundred nights. And of each new work it was said that it was more clever and grand and glorious than were even the works he had written before.

Wherever the English language was spoken, his name was an honoured household word. Wherever he went, he was fêted and lionised and cheered. Descriptions of his charming house, of his charming sayings and doings, of his charming self, were in every newspaper.

Shakespeare was not one-half so famous in his day as —— is in his.

Fortunately, he happened to be still in town; and on

being ushered into his sumptuously-furnished study, I found him sitting before one of the windows, smoking an after-dinner cigar.

He offered me one from the same box. ——'s cigars are not to be refused. I know he pays half-a-crown a-piece for them by the hundred; so I accepted, lit up, and, sitting down opposite to him, told him my trouble.

He did not answer immediately after I had finished; and I was just beginning to think that he could not have been listening, when — with his eyes looking out through the open window to where, beyond the smoky city, it seemed as if the sun, in passing through, had left the gates of the sky ajar behind him — he took his cigar from his lips, and said:

"Do you want a real pathetic story? I can tell you one if you do. It is not very long, but it is sad enough."

He spoke in so serious a tone that almost any reply seemed out of place and I remained silent.

"It is the story of a man who lost his own self," he continued, still looking out upon the dying light, as though he read the story there, "who stood by the death-bed of himself, and saw himself slowly die, and knew that he was dead — for ever.

"Once upon a time there lived a poor boy. He had little in common with other children. He loved to wander by himself, to think and dream all day. It wasd not that he was morose, or did not care for his comrades, only that something within kept whispering to his childish heart that he had deeper lessons to comprehend than his schoolmates had. And an unseen hand would lead him away into the solitude where alone he could learn their meaning.

"Ever amid the babel of the swarming street, would he hear strong, silent voices, speaking to him as he walked, telling him of the work that would one day

be entrusted to his hands,
— work for God, such as
is given to only the very
few to do, work for the
helping of God's children
in the world, for the
making of them stronger
and truer and higher; —
and, in some dimly-
lighted corner, where for
a moment they were
alone, he would stand
and raise his boyish
hands to Heaven, and
thank God for this great
promised gift of noble
usefulness, and pray that

he might ever prove worthy of the trust; and, in the joy
of his coming work, the little frets of life floated like
drift-wood on a deepening river; and as he grew, the
voices spoke to him ever more plaintly, until he saw his
work before him clearly, as a traveller on the hill-top
sees the pathway through the vale.

"And so the years passed, and he became a man, and
his labour lay ready to his hand.

"And then a foul demon came and tempted him —
the demon that has killed many a better man before,
that will kill many a great man yet — the demon of
wordly success. And the demon whispered evil words
into his ear, and, God forgive him! — he listened.

"'Of what good to *you*, think you, will it be, your
writing mighty truths and noble thoughts? What will the
world pay for *them*? What has ever been the reward of
the earth's greatest teachers and poets — the men who
have given their lives to the best service of mankind —

but neglect and scorn and poverty? Look around! what are the wages of the few earnest workers of today but a pauper's pittance, compared with the wealth that is showered down on those who jig to the tune that the crowd shouts for? Aye, the true singers are honoured when they are dead — those that are remembered; and the thoughts from their brains once fallen, whether they themselves are remembered or not, stir, with ever-widening circles to all time, the waters of human life. But of what use is that to themselves, who starved? You have talent, genius. Riches, luxury, power can be yours — soft beds and dainty foods. You can be great in the greatness that the world can see, famous with fame your own ears will hear. Work for the world, and the world will pay you promptly; the wages the gods give are long delayed.'

"And the demon prevailed over him, and he fell.

"And, instead of being the servant of God, he became the slave of men. And he wrote for the multitude what they wanted to hear, and the multitude applauded and flung money to him, and as he would stoop to pick it up, he would grin and touch his cap, and tell them how generous and noble they were.

"And the spirit of the artist that is handmaiden to the spirit of the prophet departed from him, and he grew into the clever huckster, the smart tradesman, whose only desire was to discover the public taste that he might pander to it.

"'Only tell me what it is you like,' he would cry in his heart, 'that I may write it for you, good people! Will you have again the old lies? Do you still love the old dead conventions, the worn-out formulas of life, the rotting weeds of evil thoughts that keep the fresh air from the flowers?

"'Shall I sing again to you the childish twaddle you

have heard a million times before? Shall I defend for you the wrong, and call it right? Shall I stab Truth in the back for you, or praise it?

"'How shall I flatter you today, and in what way tomorrow and the next day? Only tell me what you wish me to say, what you wish me to think, that I may say it and think it, good people, and so get your pence and your plaudits!'

"Thus he became rich and famous and great; and had fine clothes to wear and rich foods to eat, as the demon had promised him, and servants to wait on him, and horses, and carriages to ride in; and he would have been happy — as happy as such things can make a man — only that at the bottom of his desk there lay (and he had never had the courage to destroy them) a little pile of faded manuscripts, written in boyish hand, that would speak to him of the memory of a poor lad who had once paced the city's feet-worn stones, dreaming of no other greatness than that of being one of God's messengers to men, and who had died, and had been buried for all eternity, long years ago."

It was a very sad story, but not exactly the sort of sad story, I felt, that the public wants in a Christmas number. So I had to fall back upon the broken-hearted maiden, after all!

THE NEW UTOPIA

I had spent an extremely interesting evening. I had dined with some very "advanced" friends of mine at the "National Socialist Club." We had had an excellent dinner: the pheasant, stuffed with truffles, was a poem; and when I say that the '49 Chateau Lafitte was worth the price we had to pay for it, I do not see what more I can add in its favour.

After dinner, and over the cigars (I must say they do know how to stock good cigars at the National Socialist Club), we had a very instructive discussion about the coming equality of man and the nationalisation of capital.

I was not able to take much part in the argument myself, because, having been left when a boy in a position which rendered it necessary for me to earn my own living, I have never enjoyed the time and opportunity to study these questions.

But I listened very attentively while my friends explained how, for the thousands of centuries during which it had existed before they came, the world had been going on all wrong, and how, in the course of the next few years or so, they meant to put it right.

Equality of all mankind was their watchword — perfect equality in all things — equality in possessions, and equality in position and influence, and equality in duties, resulting in equality in happiness and contentment.

The world belonged to all alike, and must be equally divided. Each man's labour was the property, not of himself, but of the State which fed and clothed him, and must be applied, not to his own aggrandisement, but to the enrichment of the race.

Individual wealth — the social chain with which the few had bound the many, the bandit's pistol by which a small gang of robbers had thieved from the whole community the fruits of its labours — must be taken from the hands that too long had held it.

Social distinctions — the barriers by which the rising tide of humanity had hitherto been fretted and restrained — must be for ever swept aside. The human race must press onward to its destiny (whatever that might be), not as at present, a scattered horde, scrambling, each man for himself, over the broken ground of unequal birth and fortune — the soft sward reserved for the feet of the pampered, the cruel stones left for the feet of the cursed, — but an ordered army, marching side by side over the level plain of equity and equality.

The great bosom of our Mother Earth should nourish all her children, like and like; none should be hungry, none should have too much. The strong man should not grasp more than the weak; the clever should not scheme to seize more than the simple. The earth was man's, and the fulness thereof; and among all mankind it should be portioned out in even shares. All men were equal by the laws of Nature, and must be made equal by the laws of man.

With inequality comes misery, crime, sin, selfishness, arrogance, hypocrisy. In a world in which all men were equal, there would exist no temptation to evil, and our natural nobility would assert itself.

When all men were equal, the world would be Heaven — freed from the degrading despotism of God.

We raised our glasses and drank to EQUALITY, sacred EQUALITY; and then ordered the waiter to bring us Green Chartreuse and more cigars.

I went home very thoughtful. I did not go to sleep for a long while; I lay awake; thinking over this vision of a new world that had been presented to me.

How delightful life would be, if only the scheme of my socialistic friends could be carried out. There would be no more of this struggling and striving against each other, no more jealousy, no more disappointment, no more fear of poverty! The State would take charge of us from the hour we were born until we died, and provide for all our wants from the cradle to the coffin, both inclusive, and we should need to give no thought even to the matter. There would be no more hard work (three hours' labour a day would be the limit, according to our calculations, that the State would require from each adult citizen, and nobody would be allowed to do more — *I* should not be allowed to do more) — no poor to pity, no rich to envy — no one to look down upon us, no one for us to look down upon (not quite so pleasant this latter reflection) — all our life ordered and arranged for us — nothing to think about except the glorious destiny (whatever that might be) of Humanity!

Then thought crept away to sport in chaos, and I slept.

*   *   *   *

When I awoke, I found myself lying under a glass case, in a high, cheerless room. There was a label over my head; I turned and read it. It ran as follows:

"MAN — ASLEEP.

"PERIOD — 19TH CENTURY.

"THIS MAN WAS FOUND ASLEEP IN A HOUSE IN LONDON, AFTER THE GREAT SOCIAL REVOLUTION OF 1899. FROM THE ACCOUNT GIVEN BY THE LANDLADY OF THE HOUSE, IT WOULD APPEAR THAT HE HAD ALREADY, WHEN DISCOVERED, BEEN ASLEEP FOR OVER TEN YEARS (SHE HAVING FORGOTTEN TO CALL HIM). IT WAS DECIDED, FOR SCIENTIFIC PURPOSES, NOT TO AWAKE HIM, BUT JUST TO SEE HOW LONG HE WOULD SLEEP ON, AND HE WAS ACCORDINGLY BROUGHT AND DEPOSITED IN THE 'MUSEUM OF CURIOSITIES,' ON FEBRUARY 11TH, 1900."

"Visitors are requested not to squirt water through the air-holes."

An intelligent-looking old gentleman, who had been arranging some stuffed lizards in an adjoining case, came over and took the cover off me.

"What's the matter?" he asked; "anything disturbed you?"

"No," I said; "I always wake up like this, when I feel I've had enough sleep. What century is this?"

"This," he said, "is the twenty-ninth century. You have been asleep for just one thousand years."

"Ah! well, I feel all the better for it," I replied, getting down off the table. "There's nothing like having one's sleep out."

"I take it you are going to do the usual thing," said the old gentleman to me, as I proceeded to put on my clothes, which had been lying beside me in the case. "You'll want me to walk round the city with you, and explain all the changes to you, while you ask questions and make silly remarks?"

"Yes," I replied, "I suppose that's what I ought to do."

"I suppose so," he muttered. "Come on, and let's get it over," and he led the way from the room.

As we went downstairs, I said:

"Well, is it all right, now?"

"Is what all right?" he replied.

"Why, the world," I answered. "A few friends of mine were arranging, just before I went to bed, to take it to pieces and fix it up again properly. Have they got it all right by this time? Is everybody equal now, and sin and sorrow and all that sort of thing done away with?"

"Oh, yes," replied my guide; "you'll find everything all right now. We've been working away pretty hard at things while you've been asleep. We've just got this earth about perfect now, I should say. Nobody is allowed to do anything wrong or silly; and as for equality, tadpoles ain't in it with us."

(He talked in rather a vulgar manner, I thought; but I did not like to reprove him.)

We walked out into the city. It was very clean and very quiet. The streets, which were designated by numbers, ran out from each other at right angles, and all presented exactly the same appearance. There were no horses or carriages about; all the traffic was conducted by electric cars. All the people that we met wore a quiet grave expression, and were so much like each other as to give one the idea that they were all members of the same family. Everyone was dressed, as was also my guide, in a pair of grey trousers, and a grey tunic, buttoning tight round the neck and fastened round the waist by a belt. Each man was clean shaven, and each man had black hair.

I said:

"Are all these men twins?"

"Twins! Good gracious, no!" answered my guide. "Whatever made you fancy that?"

"Why, they all look so much alike," I replied; "and they've all got black hair!"

"Oh; that's the regulation colour for hair," explained my companion: "we've all got black hair. If a man's hair is not black naturally, he has to have it dyed black."

"Why?" I asked.

"Why!" retorted the old gentleman, somewhat irritably. "Why, I thought you understood that all men were now equal. What would become of our equality if one man or woman were allowed to swagger about in golden hair, while another had to put up with carrots? Men have not only got to be equal in these happy days, but to look it, as far as can be. By causing all men to be clean shaven, and all men and women to have black hair cut the same length, we obviate, to a certain extent, the errors of Nature."

I said:

"Why black?"

He said he did not know, but that was the colour which had been decided upon.

"Who by?" I asked.

"By THE MAJORITY," he replied, raising his hat and lowering his eyes, as if in prayer.

We walked further, and passed more men. I said:

"Are there no women in this city?"

"Women!" exclaimed my guide. "Of course there are. We've passed hundreds of them!"

"I thought I knew a woman when I saw one," I observed; "but I can't remember noticing any."

"Why, there go two, now," he said, drawing my attention to a couple of persons near to us, both dressed in the regulation grey trousers and tunics.

"How do you know they are women?" I asked.

"Why, you see the metal numbers that everybody wears on their collar?"

"Yes: I was just thinking what a number of policemen you had, and wondering where the other people were!"

'Well, the even numbers are women; the odd numbers are men."

"How very simple," I remarked. "I suppose after a little practice you can tell one sex from the other almost at a glance?"

"Oh yes," he replied, "if you want to."

We walked on in silence for a while. And then I said:

"Why does everybody have a number?"

"To distinguish him by," answered my companion.

"Don't people have names, then?"

"No."

"Why?"

"Oh! there was so much inequality in names. Some people were called Montmorency, and they looked down on the Smiths; and the Smythes did not like mixing with the Joneses: so, to save further bother, it was decided to abolish names altogether, and to give everybody a number."

"Did not the Montmorencys and the Smythes object."

"Yes: but the Smiths and Joneses were in THE MAJORITY."

"And did not the Ones and Twos look down upon the Threes and Fours, and so on?"

"At first, yes. But, with the abolition of wealth, numbers lost their value, except for industrial purposes and for double acrostics, and now No. 100 does not consider himself in any way superior to No. 1,000,000."

I had not washed when I got up, there being no conveniences for doing so in the Museum, and I was beginning to feel somewhat hot and dirty. I said:

"Can I wash myself anywhere?"

He said:

"No; we are not allowed to wash ourselves. You must wait until half-past four, and then you will be washed for tea."

"*Be* washed!" I cried. "Who by?"

"The State."

He said that they had found they could not maintain their equality when people were allowed to wash themselves. Some people washed three or four times a day, while others never touched soap and water from one year's end to the other, and in consequence there got to be two distinct classes, the Clean and the Dirty. All the old class prejudices began to be revived. The clean despised the dirty, and the dirty hated the clean. So, to end dissension, the State decided to do the washing itself, and each citizen was now washed twice a day by government-appointed officials; and private washing was prohibited.

I noticed that we passed no houses as we went along, only block after block of huge, barrack-like buildings, all of the same size and shape. Occasionally, at a corner, we came across a smaller building, labelled "Museum," "Hospital," "Debating Hall," "Bath," "Gymnasium," "Academy of Sciences," "Exhibition of Industries," "School of Talk," &c., &c.; but never a house.

I said:

"Doesn't anybody live in this town?"

He said:

"You do ask silly questions; upon my word, you do. Where do you think they live?"

I said:

"That's just what I've been trying to think. I don't see any houses anywhere!"

He said:

"We don't need houses — not houses such as you are thinking of. We are socialistic now; we live together in fraternity and equality. We live in these blocks that you see. Each block accommodates one thousand citizens. It contains one thousand beds — one hundred in each room — and bath-rooms and dressing-rooms in proportion, a dining-hall and kitchens. At seven o'clock every morning a bell is rung, and every one rises and tidies up his bed. At seven-thirty they go into the dressing-rooms, and are washed and shaved and have their hair done. At eight o'clock breakfast is served in the dining-hall. It comprises a pint of oatmeal porridge and half-a-pint of warm milk for each adult citizen. We are all strict vegetarians now. The vegetarian vote inceased enormously during the last century, and their organisation being very perfect, they have been able to dictate every election for the past fifty years. At one o'clock another bell is rung, and the people return to dinner, which consists of beans and stewed fruits, with rolly-polly pudding twice a week, and plum-duff on Saturdays. At five o'clock there is tea, and at ten the lights are put out and everybody goes to bed. We are all equal, and we all live alike — clerk and scavenger, tinker and apothecary — all together in fraternity and liberty. The men live in blocks on this side of the town, and the women are at the other end of the city."

"Where are the married people kept?" I asked.

"Oh, there are no married couples," he replied; "we abolished marriage two hundred years ago. You see, married life did not work at all well with our system. Domestic life, we found, was thoroughly anti-socialistic in its tendencies. Men thought more of their wives and families than they did of the State. They wished to labour for the benefit of their little circle of beloved ones rather than for the good of the community. They cared more for the future of their children than for the Destiny of Humanity. The ties of love and blood bound men together fast in little groups instead of in one great whole. Before considering the advancement of the human race, men considered the advancement of their kith and kin. Before striving for the greatest happiness of the greatest number, men strove for the happiness of the few who were near and dear to them. In secret, men and women hoarded up and laboured and denied themselves, so as, in secret, to give some little extra gift of joy to their beloved. Love stirred the vice of ambition in men's hearts. To win the smiles of the women they loved, to leave a name behind them that their children might be proud to bear, men sought to raise themselves above the general level, to do some deed that should make the world look up to them and honour them above their fellow-men, to press a deeper footprint than another's upon the dusty high-way of the age. The fundamental principles of Socialism were being daily thwarted and contemned. Each house was a revolutionary centre for the propagation of individualism and personality. From the warmth of each domestic hearth grew up the vipers, Comradeship and Independence, to sting the State and poison the minds of men.

"The doctrines of equality were openly disputed. Men, when they loved a woman, thought her superior to every other woman, and hardly took any pains to disguise their opinion. Loving wives believed their husbands to be wiser and braver and better than all other men. Mothers laughed at the idea of their children being in no way superior to other children. Children imbibed the hideous heresy that their father and mother were the best father and mother in the world.

"From whatever point you looked at it, the Family stood forth as our foe. One man had a charming wife and two sweet-tempered children; his neighbour was married to a shrew, and was the father of eleven noisy, ill-dispositioned brats — where was the equality?

"Again, wherever the Family existed, there hovered, ever contending, the angels of Joy and Sorrow; and in a world where joy and sorrow are known, Equality cannot live. One man and woman, in the night, stand weeping beside a little cot. On the other side of the lath-and-plaster, a fair young couple, hand in hand, are laughing at the silly antics of a grace-faced, gurgling baby. What is poor Equality doing?

"Such things could not be allowed. Love, we saw, was our enemy at every turn. He made equality impossible. He brought joy and pain, and peace and suffering in his train. He disturbed men's beliefs, and imperilled the Destiny of Humanity; so we abolished him and all his works.

"Now there are no marriages, and, therefore, no domestic troubles; no wooing, therefore, no heartaching; no loving, therefore no sorrowing; no kisses and no tears.

"We all live together in equality free from the troubling of joy or pain."

I said:

"It must be very peaceful; but, tell me — I ask the question merely from a scientific standpoint — how do you keep up the supply of men and women?"

He said:

"Oh, that's simple enough. How did you, in your day, keep up the supply of horses and cows? In the spring, so many children, according as the State requires, are arranged for, and carefully bred, under medical supervision. When they are born, they are taken away from their mothers (who, else, might grow to love them), and brought up in the public nurseries and schools until they are fourteen. They are then examined by State-appointed inspectors, who decide what calling they shall be brought up to, and to such calling they are thereupon apprenticed. At twenty they take their rank as citizens, and are entitled to a vote. No difference whatever is made between men and women. Both sexes enjoy equal privileges."

I said:

"What are the privileges?"

He said:

"Why, all that I've been telling you."

We wandered on for a few more miles, but passed nothing but street after street of these huge blocks. I said:

"Are there no shops nor stores in this town?"

"No," he replied. "What do we want with shops and stores? The State feeds us, clothes us, houses us, doctors us, washes and dresses us, cuts our corns, and buries us. What could we do with shops?"

I began to feel tired with our walk. I said:

"Can we go in anywhere and have a drink?"

He said:

"A 'drink!' What's a 'drink'? We have half-a-pint of cocoa with our dinner. Do you mean that?"

I did not feel equal to explaining the matter to him, and he evidently would not have understood me if I had; so I said:

"Yes; I meant that."

We passed a very fine-looking man a little further on, and I noticed that he only had one arm. I had noticed two or three rather big-looking men with only one arm in the course of the morning, and it struck me as curious. I remarked about it to my guide.

He said:

"Yes; when a man is much above the average size and strength, we cut one of his legs or arms off, so as to make things more equal; we lop him down a bit, as it were. Nature, you see, is somewhat behind the times; but we do what we can to put her straight."

I said:

"I suppose you can't abolish her?"

"Well, not altogether," he replied. "We only wish we could. But," he added afterwards, with pardonable pride, "we've done a good deal."

I said:

"How about an exceptionally clever man. What do you do with him?"

"Well, we are not much troubled in that way now," he answered. "We have not come across anything danger-ous in the shape of brain-power for some very consider-

able time now. When we do, we perform a surgical
operation upon the head, which softens the brain down
to the average level.

"I have sometimes thought," mused the old gentleman, "that it was a pity we could not level *up*
sometimes, instead of always levelling down; but, of
course that is impossible."

I said:

"Do you think it right of you to cut these people up,
and tone them down, in this manner?"

He said:

"Of course, it is right."

"You seem very cock-sure about the matter," I
retorted. "Why is it 'of course' right?"

"Because it is done by THE MAJORITY."

"How does that make it right?" I asked.

"A MAJORITY can do no wrong," he answered.

"Oh! is that what the people who are lopped think?"

"They!" he replied, evidently astonished at the
question. "Oh, they are in the minority, you know."

"Yes; but even the minority has a right to its arms
and legs and heads, hasn't it?"

"A minority has NO rights," he answered.

I said:

"It's just as well to belong to the Majority, if you're
thinking of living here, isn't it?"

He said:

"Yes; most of our people do. They seem to think it
more convenient."

I was finding the town somewhat uninteresting, and I
asked if we could not go into the country for a change.

My guide said:

"Oh, yes, certainly;" but did not think I should care
much for it.

"Oh! but it used to be so beautiful in the country," I

urged, "before I went to bed. There were great green trees, and grassy, wind-waved meadows, and little rose-decked cottages, and ——"

"Oh, we've changed all that," interrupted the old gentleman; "it is all one huge market-garden now, divided by roads and canals cut at right angles to each other. There is no beauty in the country now whatever. We have abolished beauty; it interfered with our equality. It was not fair that some people should live among lovely scenery, and others upon barren moors. So we have made it all pretty much alike everywhere now, and no place can lord it over another."

"Can a man emigrate into any other country?" I asked; "it doesn't matter what country — *any* other country would do."

"Oh, yes, if he likes," replies my companion; "but why should he? All lands are exactly the same. The whole world is all one people now — one language, one law, one life."

"Is there no variety, no change anywhere." I asked. "What do you do for pleasure, for recreation? Are there any theatres?"

"No," responded my guide. "We had to abolish theatres. The histrionic temperament seemed utterly unable to accept the principles of equality. Each actor thought himself the best actor in the world, and superior, in fact, to most other people altogether. I don't know whether it was the same in your day?"

"Exactly the same," I answered, "but we did not take any notice of it."

"Ah! we did," he replied, "and, in consequence, shut the theatres up. Besides, our White Ribbon Vigilance Society said that all places of amusement were vicious and degrading; and being an energetic and stout-winded band, they soon won THE MAJORITY over to their views; and so all amusements are prohibited now."

I said: "Are you allowed to read books?"

"Well," he answered, "there are not many written. You see, owing to our all living such perfect lives, and there being no wrong, or sorrow, or joy, or hope, or love, or grief in the world, and everything being so regular and so proper, there is really nothing much to write about — except, of course, the Destiny of Humanity."

"True!" I said, "I see that. But what of the old works, the classics? You had Shakespeare, and Scott, and Thackeray, and there were one or two little things of my own that were not half-bad. What have you done with all those?"

"Oh, we have burned all those old works," he said. "They were full of the old, wrong notions of the old wrong, wicked times, when men were merely slaves and beasts of burden."

He said all the old paintings and sculptures had been likewise destroyed, partly for the same reason, and partly because they were considered improper by the White Ribbon Vigilance Society, which was a great power now; while all new art and literature were forbidden, as such things tended to undermine the principles of equality. They made men think, and the men that thought grew cleverer than those that did not want to think; and those that did not want to think naturally objected to this, and being in THE MAJORITY, objected to some purpose.

He said that, from like considerations, there were no sports or games permitted. Sports and games caused competition, and competition led to inequality.

I said:

"How long do your citizens work each day?"

"Three hours," he answered; "after that, all the

remainder of the day belongs to ourselves."

"Ah! that is just what I was coming to," I remarked. "Now what do you do with yourselves during those other twenty-one hours?"

"Oh, we rest."

"What! for the whole twenty-one hours?"

"Well, rest and think and talk."

"What do you think and talk about?"

"Oh! Oh, about how wretched life must have been in the old times, and about how happy we are now, and — and — oh, and the Destiny of Humanity!"

"Don't you ever get sick of the Destiny of Humanity?"

"No, not much."

"And what do you understand by it? What *is* the Destiny of Humanity, do you think?"

"Oh! — why to — to go on being like we are now, only more so — everybody more equal, and more things done by electricity, and everybody to have two votes instead of one, and ——"

"Thank you. That will do. Is there anything else that you think of? Have you got a religion?"

"Oh, yes."

"And you worship a Good?"

"Oh, yes."

"What do you call him?"

"THE MAJORITY."

"One question more —— You don't mind my asking you all these questions, by-the-by, do you?"

"Oh, no. This is all part of my three hours' labour for the State."

"Oh, I'm glad of that. I should not like to feel that I was encroaching on your time for rest; but what I wanted to ask was, do many of the people here commit suicide?"

"No; such a thing never occurs to them."

I looked at the faces of the men and women that were passing. There was a patient, almost pathetic, expression upon them all. I wondered where I had seen that look before; it seemed familiar to me.

All at once I remembered. It was just the quiet, troubled, wondering expression that I had always noticed upon the faces of the horses and oxen that we used to breed and keep in the old world.

No. These people would *not* think of suicide.

*   *   *   *

Strange! how very dim and indistinct all the faces are growing around me! And where is my guide? and why am I sitting on the pavement? and — hark! surely that is the voice of Mrs. Biggles, my old land-lady. Has *she* been asleep a thousand years, too? She says it is twelve o'clock — only twelve? and I'm not to be washed till half-past four; and I do feel so stuffy and hot, and my head is aching. Hulloa! why, I'm in bed! Has it all been a dream? And am I back in the nineteenth century?

Through the open window I hear the rush and roar of old life's battle. Men are fighting, striving, working, carving out each man his own life with the sword of strength and will. Men are laughing, grieving, loving, doing wrong deeds, doing great deeds, — falling, struggling, helping one another — living!

And I have a good deal more than three hours' work to do today, and I meant to be up at seven; and, oh dear! I do wish I had not smoked so many strong cigars last night!

DREAMS

The most extraordinary dream I ever had was one in which I fancied that, as I was going into a theatre, the cloak-room attendant stopped me in the lobby and insisted on my leaving my legs behind me.

I was not surprised; indeed, my acquaintanceship with theatre harpies would prevent my feeling any surprise at such a demand, even in my waking moments; but I was, I must honestly confess, considerably annoyed. It was not the payment of the cloak-room fee that I so much minded, — I offered to give that to the man then and there. It was the parting with my legs that I objected to.

I said I had never heard of such a rule being attempted to be put in force at any respectable theatre before, and that I considered it a most absurd and vexatious regulation. I also said I should write to *The Times* about it.

The man replied that he was very sorry, but that

those were his instructions. People complained that they could not get to and from their seats comfortably, because other people's legs were always in the way; and it had, therefore, been decided that, in future, everybody should leave their legs outside.

It seemed to me that the management, in making this order, had clearly gone beyond their legal right; and under ordinary circumstances I should have disputed it. Being present, however, more in the character of a guest than in that of a patron, I hardly liked to make a disturbance; and so I sat down and meekly prepared to comply with the demand.

I had never before known that the human leg did unscrew. I had always thought it was a fixture. But the man showed me how to undo them, and I found that they came off quite easily.

The discovery did not surprise me any more than the original request that I should take them off had done. Nothing does surprise one in a dream.

I dreamed once that I was going to be hanged; but I was not at all surprised about it. Nobody was. My relations came to see me off, I thought, and to wish me "Good-bye!" They all came, and were all very pleasant; but they were not in the least astonished — not one of them. Everybody appeared to regard the coming tragedy as one of the most-naturally-to-be-expected things in the world.

They bore the calamity, besides, with an amount of stoicism that would have done credit to a Spartan father. There was no fuss, no scene. On the contrary, an atmosphere of mild cheerfulness prevailed.

Yet they were very kind. Somebody — an uncle, I think — left me a packet of sandwiches and a little something in a flask, in case, as he said, I should feel peckish on the scaffold.

It is "those twin-gaolers of the daring" thought, Knowledge and Experience, that teach us surprise. We are surprised and incredulous when, in novels and plays, we come across good men and women, because Knowledge and Experience have taught us how rare and problematical is the existence of such people. In waking life, my friends and relations would, of course, have been surprised at hearing that I had committed a murder, and was, in consequence, about to be hanged, because Knowledge and Experience would have taught them that, in a country where the law is powerful and the police alert, the Christian citizen is usually pretty successful in withstanding the voice of temptation, prompting him to commit crime of an illegal character.

But into Dreamland, Knowledge and Experience do not enter. They stay without, together with the dull, dead clay of which they form a part; while the freed brain, released from their narrowing tutelage, steals softly past the ebon gate, to wanton at its own sweet will among the mazy paths that wind through the garden of Persephone.

Nothing that it meets with in that eternal land astonishes it, because, unfettered by the dense conviction of our waking mind, that nought outside the ken of our own vision can in this universe be, all things to it are possible and even probable. In dreams, we fly and wonder not: except that we never flew before. We go naked, yet are not ashamed, though we mildly wonder what the police are about that they do not stop us. We converse with our dead, and think it was unkind that they did not come back to us before. In dreams, there happens that which human language cannot tell. In dreams, we see "the light that never was on sea or land," we hear the sounds that never yet were heard by waking ears.

It is only in sleep that true imagination ever stirs within us. Awake, we never imagine anything; we merely alter, vary, or transpose. We give another twist to the kaleidoscope of the things we see around us, and obtain another pattern; but not one of us has ever added one tiniest piece of new glass to the toy.

A Dean Swift sees one race of people smaller, and another race of people larger, than the race of people that live down his own street. And he also sees a land where the horses take the place of men, and men take the place of horses. A Bulwer Lytton lays the scene of one of his novels inside the earth instead of outside. A Rider Haggard introduces us to a lady whose age is a few years more than the average woman would care to confess to; and pictures crabs larger than the usual shilling or eighteen-penny size. The number of so-called imaginative writers who visit the moon is legion, and for all the novelty that they find, when they get there, they might just as well have gone to Putney. Others are continually drawing for us visions of the world one hundred or one thousand years hence. There is always a depressing absence of human nature about the place; so much so, that one feels great consolation in the thought, while reading, that we ourselves shall be comfortably dead and buried before the picture can be realised. In these prophesied Utopias everybody is painfully good and clean and happy, and all the work is done by electricity.

There is somewhat too much electricity, for my taste, in these worlds to come. One is reminded of those pictorial enamel-paint advertisements that one sees about so often now, in which all the members of an extensive household are represented as gathered together in one room, spreading enamel-paint over everything they can lay their hands upon. The old man is on a step-ladder, daubing the walls and ceiling with "cuckoo's-egg green," while the parlourmaid and the cook are on their knees, painting the floor with "sealing-wax red." The old lady is doing the picture-frames in "terra cotta." The eldest daughter and her young man are making sly love in a corner over a pot of "high-art yellow," with which, so soon as they have finished wasting their time, they will, it is manifest, proceed to elevate the piano. Younger brothers and sisters are busy freshening up the chairs and tables with "strawberry-jam pink" and "jubilee magenta". Every blessed thing in that room is being coated with enamel paint, from the sofa to the fireirons, from the sideboard to the eight-day clock. If there is any paint left over, it will be used up for the family bible and the canary.

It is claimed for this invention that a little child can make as much mess with it as can a grown-up person, and so all the children of the family are represented in the picture as hard at work, enamelling whatever few articles of furniture and household use the grasping selfishness of their elders has spared to them. One is painting the toasting fork a "skim-milk blue," while another is giving aesthetical value to the Dutch oven by means of a new shade of art green. The bootjack is being renovated in "old gold," and the baby is sitting on the floor, smothering its own cradle with "flush-upon-a-maiden's-cheek peach colour."

One feels that the thing is being overdone. That family, before another month is gone, will be among the strongest opponents of enamel paint that the century had produced. Enamel paint will be the ruin of that once happy home. Enamel paint has a cold, glassy, cynical appearance. Its presence everywhere about the place will begin to irritate the old man in the course of a week or so. He will call it, "This damn'd sticky stuff!"

and will tell the wife that he wonders she didn't paint herself and the children with it while she was about it. She will reply, in an exasperatingly quiet tone of voice, that she does like that! Perhaps he will say next, that she did not warn him against it, and tell him what an idiot he was making of himself, spoiling the whole house with his foolish fads. Each one will persist that it was the other one who first suggested the absurdity, and they will sit up in bed and quarrel about it every night for a month.

The children, having acquired a taste for smudging the concoction about, and there being nothing else left untouched in the house, will try to enamel the cat; and then there will be bloodshed, and broken windows, and spoiled infants, and sorrows and yells. The smell of the paint will make everybody ill; and the servants will give notice. Tradesmen's boys will lean up against places that are not dry and get their clothes enamelled, and claim compensation. And the baby will suck the paint off its cradle and have fits.

But the person that will suffer most will, of course, be the eldest daughter's young man. The eldest daughter's young man is always unfortunate. He means well, and he tries hard. His great ambition is to make the family love him. But Fate is ever against him, and he only succeeds in gaining their undisguised contempt. The fact of his being "gone" on their Emily is, of itself, naturally sufficient to stamp him as an imbecile in the eyes of Emily's brothers and sisters. The father finds him slow, and thinks the girl might have done better; while the best that his future mother-in-law (his sole supporter) can say for him is, that he seems steady.

There is only one thing that prompts the family to tolerate him, and that is the reflection that he is going to take Emily away from them.

On that understanding they put up with him.

The eldest daughter's young man, in this particular case, will, you may depend upon it, choose that exact moment when the baby's life is hovering in the balance, and the cook is waiting for her wages with her box in the hall, and a coal-heaver is at the front door with a policeman, making a row about the damage to his  trousers, to come in, smiling, with a specimen pot of some new high art, squashed-tomato-shade enamel paint,

 and suggest that they should try it on the old man's pipe.

Then Emily will go off into hysterics, and Emily's male progenitor will firmly but quietly lead that ill-starred yet true-hearted young man to the public side of the garden-gate; and the engagement will be "off."

Too much of anything is a mistake, as the man said when his wife presented him with four new healthy children in one day. We should practise moderation in all matters. A little enamel paint would have been good. They might have enamelled the house inside and out, and have left the furniture alone. Or they might have coloured the furniture, and let the house be. But an entirely and completely enamelled home — a home, such as enamel-paint manufacturers love to picture on their advertisements, over which the yearning eye wanders in vain, seeking one single square inch of unenamelled matter — is, I am convinced, a mistake. It may be a home that, as the testimonials assure us, will easily wash. It may be an "artistic" home; but the average man is not yet educated up to the appreciation of it. The average man does not care for high art. At a certain point, the average man gets sick of high art.

So, in these coming Utopias, in which our unhappy grandchildren will have to drag out their colourless existence, there will be too much electricity. They will grow to loathe electricity.

Electricity is going to light them, warm them, carry them, doctor them, cook for them, execute them, if necessary. They are going to be weaned on electricity, ruled and regulated and guided by electricity, buried by electricity. I may be wrong, but I rather think they are going to be hatched by electricity.

In the new world of our progressionist teachers, it is electricity that is the real motive-power. The men and women are only marionettes — worked by electricity.

But it was not to speak of the electricity in them, but of the originality in them, that I referred to these works of fiction. There is no originality in them whatever. Human thought is incapable of originality. No man ever yet imagined a new thing — only some variation or extension of an old thing.

The sailor, when he was asked what he would do with a fortune, promptly replied:

"Buy all the rum and 'baccy there is in the world."

"And what after that?" they asked him.

"Eh?"

"What would you buy after that — after you had bought all the rum and tobacco there was in the world? — what would you buy then?"

"After that? Oh! um!" (a long pause). "Oh!" (with inspiration) "why, more 'baccy!"

Rum and tobacco he knew something of, and could therefore imagine about. He did not know any other luxuries, therefore he could not conceive of any others.

So if you asked one of these Utopian-dreaming gentry what, after they had secured for their world all the electricity there was in the Universe, and after every mortal thing in their ideal Paradise was done and said and thought by electricity, they could imagine as further necessary to human happiness, they would probably muse for a while, and then reply "More electricity."

They *know* electricity. They have seen the electric light, and heard of electric boats and omnibuses. They have possibly had an electric shock at a railway station for a penny.

Therefore, knowing that electricity does three things, they can go on and "imagine" electricity doing three hundred things, and the very great ones among them can imagine it doing three thousand things; but for them, or anybody else, to imagine a new force, totally unconnected with and different from anything yet known in nature would be utterly impossible.

Human thought is not a firework, ever shooting off fresh forms and shapes as it burns: it is a tree, growing very slowly — you can watch it long and see no movement — very silently, unnoticed. It was planted in the world many thousand years ago, a tiny, sickly plant. And men guarded it and tended it, and gave up life and fame to aid its growth. In the hot days of their youth, they came to the gate of the garden and knocked, begging to be let in, and to be counted among the gardeners. And their young companions without called to them to come back, and play the man with bow and spear, and win sweet smiles from rosy lips, and take their part amid the feast, and dance, not stoop with wrinkled brows, at weaklings' work. And the passers-by mocked them and called shame, and others cried out to stone them. And still they stayed there labouring, that the tree might grow a little, and they died and were forgotten.

And the tree grew fair and strong. The storms of ignorance passed over it, and harmed it not. The fierce fires of superstition soared around it; but men leapt into the flames and beat them back, perishing, and the tree grew.

With the sweat of their brow have men nourished its green leaves. Their tears have moistened the earth about it. With their blood they have watered its roots.

The seasons have come and passed, and the tree has grown and flourished. And its branches have spread far and high, and ever fresh shoots are bursting forth and ever new leaves unfolding to the light. But they are all part of the one tree — the tree that was planted on the first birthday of the human race. The stem that bears them springs from the gnarled old trunk that was green and soft when white-haired Time was a little child; the sap that feeds them is drawn up through the roots that twine and twist about the bones of the ages that are dead.

The human mind can no more produce an original thought than a tree can bear an original fruit. As well might one cry for an original note in music as expect an original idea from a human brain.

One wishes our friends, the critics, would grasp this simple truth, and leave off clamouring for the impossible, and being shocked because they do not get it.

When a new book is written, the high-class critic opens it with feelings of faint hope, tempered by strong conviction of coming disappointment. As he pores over the pages, his brow darkens with virtuous indignation, and his lip curls with the God-like contempt that the exceptionally great critic ever feels for everybody in this world, who is not yet dead. Buoyed up by a touching, but toally fallacious, belief that he is performing a public duty, and that the rest of the community is waiting in breathless suspense to learn his opinion of the work in question, before forming any judgement concerning it themselves, he, nevertheless, wearily struggles through about a third of it. Then his long-suffering soul revolts, and he flings it aside with a cry of despair.

"Why, there is no originality whatever in this," he says. "This book is taken bodily from the Old Testament. It is the story of Adam and Eve all over again. The hero is a mere man! with two arms, two legs, and a head (so called). Why, it is only Moses's Adam under another name! And the heroine is nothing but a woman! and she is described as beautiful, and as having long hair. The author may call her 'Angelina,' or any other name he chooses; but he has evidently, whether he acknowledges it or not, copied her direct from Eve. The characters are barefaced plagiarisms from the book of Genesis! Oh! to find an author with originality!"

One spring I went a walking tour in the country. It was a glorious spring. Not the sort of spring they give us in these miserable times, under this shameless government — a mixture of East wind, blizzard, snow, rain, slush, fog, frost, hail, sleet, and thunder-storms — but a sunny, blue-sky'd, joyous spring, such as we used to have regularly every year when I was a young man, and things were different.

It was an exceptionally beautiful spring, even for

those golden days; and, as I wandered through the waking land, and saw the dawning of the coming green and watched the blush upon the hawthorn hedge, deepening each day beneath the kisses of the sun, and looked up at the proud old mother trees, dandling their myriad baby buds upon their strong fond arms, holding them high for the soft West wind to caress as he passed laughing by, and marked the primrose yellow creep across the carpet of the woods, and saw the new flush of the fields, and saw the new light on the hills, and heard the new-found gladness of the birds, and heard from copse and farm and meadow, the timid callings of the little new-born things, wondering to find themselves alive, and smelt the freshness of the earth, and felt the promise in the air, and felt a strong hand in the wind, my spirit rose within me. Spring had come to me also, and stirred me with a strange new life, with a strange new hope. I, too, was part of Nature, and it was Spring! Tender leaves and blossoms were unfolding from my heart. Bright flowers of love and gratitude were opening round its roots. I felt new strength in all my limbs. New blood was pulsing through my veins. Nobler thoughts and nobler longings were throbbing through my brain.

As I walked, Nature came and talked beside me, and showed me the world and myself, and the ways of God seemed clearer.

It seemed to me a pity that all the beautiful and precious thoughts and ideas that were crowding in upon me should be lost to my fellow-men, and so I pitched my tent at a little cottage, and set to work to write them down then and there as they came to me.

"It has been complained of me," I said to myself "that I do not write literary and high-class work — at least, not work that is exceptionally literary and high-class. This reproach shall be removed. I will write an article that shall be a classic. I have worked for the ordinary, every-day reader. It is right that I should do something now to improve the literature of my beloved country."

And I wrote a grand essay — though I say it who should not, though I don't see why I shouldn't — all about Spring, and the way it made you feel, and what it made you think. It was simply crowded with elevated thoughts and high-class ideas and cultured wit, was that essay. There was only one fault about that essay: it was too brilliant. It wanted commonplace relief. It would have exhausted the average reader: so much cleverness would have wearied him.

I wish I could remember some of the beautiful things in that essay, and here set them down; because then you would be able to see what they were like for yourselves, and that would be so much simpler than my explaining to you how beautiful they were. Unfortunately, however, I cannot now call to mind any of them.

I was very proud of this essay, and when I got back to town I called on a very superior friend of mine, a critic, and read it to him. I do not care for him to see any of

my usual work, because he really is a very superior person indeed, and the perusal of it appears to give him pains inside. But this article, I thought, would do him good.

"What do you think of it?" I asked, when I had finished.

"Splendid," he replied, "excellently arranged. I never know you were so well acquainted with the works of the old writers. Why, there is scarcely a classic of any note that you have not quoted from. But where — where," he added, musing, "did you get that last idea but two from? It's the only one I don't seem to remember. It isn't a bit of your own, is it?"

He said that, if so, he should advise me to leave it out. Not that it was altogether bad, but that the interpolation of a modern thought among so unique a collection of passages from the ancients seemed to spoil the scheme.

And he enunciated the various dead-and-buried gentlemen from whom he appeared to think I had collated my article.

"But," I replied, when I had recovered my astonishment sufficiently to speak, "It isn't a collection at all. It is all original. I wrote the thoughts down as they came to me. I have never read any of these people you mention, except Shakespeare."

Of course Shakespeare was bound to be among them. I am getting to dislike that man so. He is always being held up before us young authors as a model, and I do hate models. There was a model boy at our school, I remember, Henry Summers; and it was just the same there. It was continually, "Look at Henry Summers! *he* doesn't put the preposition before the verb, and spell business b-i-z!" or, "Why can't you write like Henry Summers? *He* doesn't get the ink all over the copy-book

and half-way up his back!" We got tired of this everlasting "Look at Henry Summers!" after a while, and so,
one afternoon, on the way home, a few of us lured
Henry Summers up a dark court; and when he came out
again he was not worth looking at.

Now it is perpetually, "Look at Shakespeare!" "Why
don't you write like Shakespeare?" "Shakespeare never
made that joke. Why don't you joke like Shakespeare?"

If you are in the play-writing line it is still worse for
you. "Why don't you write plays like Shakespeare's?"
they indignantly say. "Shakespeare never made his
comic man a penny steamboat captain." "Shakespeare
never made his hero address the girl as 'ducky'. Why
don't you copy Shakespeare?" If you do try to copy
Shakespeare, they tell you that you must be a fool to
attempt to imitate Shakespeare.

Oh, shouldn't I like to get Shakespeare up our street,
and punch him!

"I cannot help that," replied my critical friend — to
return to our previous question — "the germ of every
thought and idea you have got in that article can be
traced back to the writers I have named. If you doubt it,
I will get down the books, and show you the passages
for yourself."

But I declined the offer. I said I would take his word
for it, and would rather not see the passages referred to.
I felt indignant. "If," as I said, "these men — these
Platos and Socrateses and Ciceros and Sophocleses and
Aristophaneses and Aristotles and the rest of them had
been taking advantage of my absence to go about the
world spoiling my business for me, I would rather not
hear any more about them.

And I put on my hat and came out, and I have never
tried to write anything original since.

I dreamed a dream once. (It is the sort of thing a man

would dream. You cannot very well dream anything else, I know. But the phrase sounds poetical and biblical, and so I use it.) I dreamt that I was in a strange country — indeed, one might say an extraordinary country. It was ruled entirely by critics.

The people in this strange land had a very high opinion of critics — nearly as high an opinion of critics as the critics themselves had, but not, of course, quite, that not being practicable — and they had agreed to be guided in all things by the critics. I stayed some years in that land. But it was not a cheerful place to live in, so I dreamt.

There were authors in this country, at first, and they wrote books. But the critics could find nothing original in the books whatever, and said it was a pity that men, who might be usefully employed hoeing potatoes, should waste their time and the time of the critics, which was of still more importance, in stringing together a collection of platitudes, familiar to every school-boy, and dishing up old plots and stories that had already been cooked and recooked for the public until everybody had been surfeited with them.

And the writers read what the critics said, and sighed, and gave up writing books, and went off and hoed potatoes, as advised. They had no experience in hoeing potatoes, and they hoed very badly; and the people whose potatoes they hoed strongly recommended them to leave hoeing potatoes, and to go back and write books. But you can't do what everybody advises.

There were artists also in this strange world, at first, and they painted pictures, which the critics came and looked at through eyeglasses.

"Nothing whatever original in them," said the critics; "same old colours, same old perspective and form, same old sunset, same old sea and land and sky and figures.

Why do these poor men waste their time, painting pictures, when they might be so much more satisfactorily employed on ladders, painting houses?"

Nothing, by-the-by you may have noticed, troubles your critic more than the idea that the artist is wasting his time. It is the waste of time that vexes the critic: he has such an exalted idea of the value of other people's time. "Dear, dear me!" he says to himself, "why, in the time the man must have taken to paint this picture or to write this book, he might have blacked fifteen thousand pairs of boots, or have carried fifteen thousand hods of mortar up a ladder. This is how the time of the world is lost!"

It never occurs to him that, but for that picture or book, the artist would, in all probability, have been mouching about with a pipe in his mouth, getting into trouble.

It reminds me of the way people used to talk to me when I was a boy. I would be sitting, as good as gold, reading *The Pirate's Lair,* when some cultured relative would look over my shoulder and say: "Bah! what are you wasting your time with that rubbish for? Why don't you go and do something useful;" and would take the book away from me. Upon which I would get up, and go out to "do something useful?" and would come home an hour afterwards, looking like a bit out of a battle picture, having tumbled through the roof of Farmer Bates's greenhouse and killed a cactus, though totally unable to explain how I cam to be *on* the roof of Farmer Bates's greenhouse. They had much better have left me alone, lost in *The Pirate's Lair!*

The artists in this land of which I dreamt left off painting pictures, after hearing what the critics said, and purchased ladders, and went off and painted houses.

Because, you see, this country of which I dreamt was

not one of those vulgar, ordinary countries, such as exist in the waking world, where people let the critics talk as much as ever they like, and nobody pays the slightest attention to what they say. Here, in this strange land, the critics were taken seriously, and their advice followed. As for the poets and sculptors, they were very soon shut up. The idea of any educated person wanting to read modern poetry when he could obtain Homer, or caring to look at any other statue while there was still some of the Venus de Medicis left, was too absurd. Poets and sculptors were only wasting their time.

What new occupation they were recommended to adopt, I forget. Some calling they knew nothing whatever about, and that they were totally unfitted for, of course.

The musicians tried their art for a little while, but they, too, were of no use. "Merely a repetition of the same notes in different combinations," said the critics. "Why will people waste their time writing unoriginal music, when they might be sweeping crossings?"

One man had written a play. I asked what the critics had said about *him*. They showed me his tomb.

Then, there being no more artists or *literateurs* or dramatists or musicians left for their beloved critics to criticise, the general public of this enlightened land said to themselves, "Why should not our critics come and criticise *us*? Criticism is useful to a man. Have we not often been told so? Look how useful it has been to the artists and writers — saved the poor fellows from wasting their time! Why shouldn't *we* have some of its benefits?"

They suggested the idea to the critics, and the critics thought it an excellent one, and said they would undertake the job with pleasure. One must say for the critics that they never shirk work. They will sit and criticise for eighteen hours a day, if necessary, or even if quite unnecessary, for the matter of that. You can't give them too much to criticise. They will criticise everything and everybody in this world. They will criticise everything in the next world, too, when they get there. I expect poor old Pluto has a lively time with them all, as it is.

So, when a man built a house, or a farm-yard hen laid an egg, the critics were asked in to comment on it. They found that none of the houses were original. On every floor were passages that seemed mere copies from passages in other houses. They were all built on the same hackneyed plan: cellars underneath, ground floor level with the street, attic at the top. No originality anywhere!

So, likewise, with the eggs. Every egg suggested reminiscences of other eggs.

It was heartrending work.

The critics criticised all things. When a young couple fell in love, they each, before thinking of marriage, called upon the critics for a criticism of the other one.

Needless to say that, in the result, no marriage ever came of it.

"My dear young lady," the critics would say, after the inspection had taken place, "I can discover nothing new whatever about the young man. You would simply be wasting your time in marrying him." Or, to the young man it would be:

"Oh dear, no! Nothing attractive about the girl at all. Who on earth gave you that notion? Simply a lovely face and figure, angelic disposition, beautiful mind, staunch heart, noble character. Why, there must have been nearly a dozen such girls born into the world since its creation. You would be only wasting your time loving her."

They criticised the birds for their hackneyed style of singing, and the flowers for their hackneyed scents and colours. They complained of the weather that it lacked originality — (true, they had not lived out an English spring) — and found fault with the Sun because of the sameness of his methods.

They criticised the babies. When a fresh infant was published in a house, the critics would call in a body to pass their judgement upon it, and the young mother would bring it down for them to sample.

"Did you ever see a child anything like that in this world before?" she would say, holding it out to them. "Isn't it a wonderful baby? *You* never saw a child with legs like that, *I* know. Nurse says he's the most extraordinary baby she ever attended. Bless him!"

But the critics did not think anything of it.

"Tut, tut," they would reply, "there is nothing extraordinary about that child — no originality whatever. Why, it's exactly like every other baby — bald head, red face, big mouth and stumpy nose. Why, that's only a weak imitation of the baby next door. It's a plagiarism, that's what your child is. You've been wasting your time, madam. If you can't do anything more original than that, we should advise you to give up the business altogether."

That was the end of criticism in that strange land.

"Oh! look here, we've had enough of you and your originality," said the people to the critics, after that. "Why, *you* are not original, when one comes to think of it, and your criticisms are not original. You've all of you been saying exactly the same thing ever since the time of Solomon. We are going to drown you and have a little peace."

"What, drown a critic!" cried the critics, "never heard of such a monstrous proceeding in our lives!"

"No, we flatter ourselves it is an original idea," replied the public, brutally. "You ought to be charmed with it. Out you come!"

So they took the critics out and drowned them, and then passed a short act, making criticism a capital offence,

After that, the art and literature of the country followed, somewhat, the methods of the quaint and curious school, but the land, notwithstanding, was a much more cheerful place to live in, I dreamt.

But I never finished telling you about the dream in which I thought I left my legs behind me, when I went into a certain theatre.

I dreamt that the ticket the man gave me for my legs was No. 19, and I was worried all through the performance for fear No. 61 should get hold of them, and leave me his instead. Mine are rather a fine pair of legs, and I am, I confess, a little proud of them — at all events, I prefer them to anybody else's. Besides, number sixty-one's might be a skinny pair, and not fit me.

It quite spoilt my evening, fretting about this.

Another extraordinary dream I had was one in which I dreamt that I was engaged to be married to my Aunt Jane. That was not, however, the extraordinary part of it: I have often known people to dream things like that. I knew a man who once dreamt that he was actually married to his own mother-in-law! He told me that never in his life had he loved the alarm clock with more deep and grateful tenderness than he did that morning. The dream almost reconciled him to being married to his real wife. They lived quite happily together, after that dream, for a few days.

No; the extraordinary part of my dream was, that I *knew* it was a dream. "What on earth will uncle say to this engagement?" I thought to myself, in my dream. "There's bound to be a row about it. We shall have a deal of trouble with uncle, I feel sure." And this thought quite troubled me until the sweet reflection came: "Ah! well, it's only a dream."

And I made up my mind that I would wake up as soon as uncle found out about the engagement, and leave him and Aunt Jane to fight the matter out between themselves.

It is a very great comfort, when the dream grows troubled and alarming, to feel that it *is* only a dream, and to know that we shall awake soon, and be none the worse for it. We can dream out the foolish perplexity with a smile then.

Sometimes the dream of life grows strangely troubled and perplexing, and then he who meets dismay the bravest is he who feels that the fretful play *is* but a dream — a brief, uneasy dream of three score years and ten, or thereabouts, from which, in a little while, he will awake — at least, he dreams so.

How dull, how impossible, life would be without dreams — waking dreams, I mean — the dreams that we call "castles in the air," built by the kindly hands of Hope! Were it not for the mirage of the oasis, drawing his footsteps ever onward, the weary traveller would lie down in the desert sand, and die. It is the mirage of distant success, of happiness that, like the bunch of carrots fastened just beyond the donkey's nose, seems always just within our reach, if only we will gallop fast enough, that makes us run so eagerly along the road of Life.

Providence, like a father with a tired child, lures us ever along the way with tales and promises, until, at the frowning gate that ends the road, we shrink back, frightened. Then, promises still more sweet he stoops and whispers in our ear, and timid yet partly reassured, and trying to hide our fears, we gather up all that is left of our little stock of hope and, trusting yet half afraid, push out our groping feet into the darkness.

THE END